Tides of Fortune

~ Pirate ~

Steven Becker

The White Marlin Press
whitemarlinpress.com

This is a work of fiction. Names, characters, places and incidents either are the product of the author's imagination or are used fictitiously . Any resemblance to any persons, living or dead, events or locales is entirely coincidental.

Booksbybecker@gmail.com
http://www.whitemarlinpress.com

Tides of Fortune

~ Pirate ~

STEVEN BECKER

Chapter One

The crew were scattered among the bonfires lit to ward off the cold Florida morning. We waited on the beach of what had become known as Gasparilla Island on the west coast of the peninsula called Florida. The men were anxious, all knowing that the next few hours would decide both their fortunes and fates. We had passed bottles of rum back and forth last night as usual, but most remained sober in order to have their wits about them. I stood on the beach searching for any sign of the captain and the treasure we were to split, but as yet he had not appeared.

I felt naked standing alone, knowing eyes were on me. As cabin boy I was usually close to the captain, should he need me, and I feared their restlessness would turn against me if he did not appear soon. I have never been sure if it was the four years I had spent by the captain's side or my own abilities that the crew respected, but they generally left me alone. In fact many often looked to me for orders rather than Rhames, the first mate. Most knew that I could read and write elevating me to the unearned status of advisor. Lately, several of the men had sought me out, asking questions that I couldn't answer; mainly what they should do and where they should go with their share of the loot. My value to them was lost if Gasparilla failed to appear.

This morning we were to divide what was left of our efforts to pirate every ship that had crossed our path over the last years. Our captain held a grudge against the Spanish, but any merchant ship had been fair prey. As I looked at the water waiting for the captain to arrive, I couldn't help but notice the glances cast toward me. They looked at me as if I knew what each man's share would be, something only Gasparilla had knowledge of - if he even did. I feared if it was not enough, there would be blood. The men's expectations were hard to judge and I was getting anxious.

Things were different these days and at least I suspected that pirates, as we were, would soon be extinct. Gone were the dens of iniquity like Port Royal in Jamaica or New Providence in the Bahamas, where men could spend their plunder freely, often going from wealthy to broke within days. It was 1821 now, and rumor had it that the United States, after defeating Britain in the War of 1812, several years ago, had its eye on becoming a sea power. And that involved eliminating piracy from its waters. The fledgling government was expanding after beating the British back for the second time and Florida was a hinderance to them. I had come across a newspaper clipping that contained a quote from Secretary of State, John Quincy Adams that said, *Florida had become a derelict open to the occupancy of every enemy, civilized or savage, of the United States, and serving no other earthly purpose than as a post of annoyance to them.* I had read the quote several times to the crew and received roars of approval There were rumors that Spain, unable to control it, was ready to cede the state to the new government and the Navy was ready to launch a fleet to eliminate our kind.

Personally, I had no other pirating experience, being liberated from my family by this very group at the age of thirteen. Gasparilla, known to his men as Gaspar, had become a father figure to me. His reputation was of a bloodthirsty buccaneer, but that was at least partially fabricated to enhance his reputation. Yes, he was a pirate, but having survived into his sixties, I knew there to be more to him than just a legend. He was also a thinker and maybe that was our bond. Gasparilla was not your typical buccaneer. His reputation for blood lust was in revenge for his past, having served in both the Spanish Navy and the court of Charles III, where he was disgraced and turned to piracy. But the facts were that he was an aristocrat and generally behaved like one. Well educated and cultured he remained aloof and a mystery to his men. We had spent hours talking and planning for the changing world and today was the result.

My thoughts were interrupted by several men running toward me. I scanned the water, finally seeing what they had in the dim light of the morning, a lone boat making its way to the shore. More men ran to the beach and waded into the water, waiting to guide the boat as it surfed the knee high waves. With four men on each side, they guided the boat and our captain to rest on the sand where more men waited to haul the craft above the water line. Gaspar eased over the side, men clapping him on the back, relieved that he had come. There had been talk that he had absconded with the majority of the treasure, leaving them with little, but as they hauled the ten chests from the boat their mood lightened. I had my doubts this was the entire treasure, having inventoried most of the boats we had taken, but I remained quiet.

"Come on boys." The captain stood on a chest and yelled to any stragglers not already there. "Time for y'all to be wealthy bastards." He jumped down and called to Rhames who stood in front of the chests with one hand on his flint lock pistol, the other on his cutlass. The crew backed away respecting the man's competence and brutality. The last of the men who had obviously partaken in an excess of rum last night wandered over.

"Nick. Come over here and bring the manifest," He called to me. We had prearranged this meeting to the last detail. I pulled the folded papers from my vest and moved next to him, ceremoniously unfolding them as he had instructed me to heighten the drama. Knowing we were the only two assembled who could read, he knew the crew would respect the mystery of what was written on the documents.

He took the two sheets and held them over his head. "This is it men," he waved the papers. "The fruits of your labor. We split it now and today we go our separate ways, all rich men."

A cheer came from the men as two of their cohorts, also preselected for their loyalty moved past Rhames and went to the chests. The men gathered closer, several carrying torches that lit the plain oak containers. The crew gasped as the lids opened one at a time, the glow of gold, silver and jewels sparkling in the light. I tensed slightly knowing that if it was going to get ugly, it was going to be now, but the captain distracted them with the manifest. In truth, it was all gibberish, just a ruse to reassure the crew that this had been planned and each would get their fair share.

I started calling the names, beginning with the lowest, skipping over myself. We had decided earlier that the captain would retain my share until we reached the mainland. There we would decide whether to stay together or go our separate ways. I was glad for his protection as any one of these men could have taken my share with a cross look. I had learned some skill with a pistol and sword, but I had never adopted their love of violence.

They started to line up, holding burlap sacks in front of them when we were interrupted by a scream.

"Ship."

The crew gathered to where the man was standing.

Chapter Two

The outline of a lone frigate was clear in the distance, working north toward Tampa. Those looking through spyglasses called out that it was flying the Union Jack - a sure sign of a merchant ship in these now American controlled waters. An argument ensued as our proclaimed retirement, just started that morning, was now threatened, but majority ruled and we made for the boats to pursue the promise of plunder. I took my place beside Gaspar in the lead boat as we rowed for our ship, the Floridablanca, and scrambled up the ropes toward the deck. No time was wasted weighing anchor and setting sail as we all watched the ship's approach. The square-rigged ship appeared to be on a port tack fighting the north wind with shortened sail, something that surely should have alarmed us. If I was navigating, I would surely hold further out to sea, away from the dangers the land held. It was not my place and I held my tongue. The lure of treasure and women overcame our good sense as we scrambled around the deck preparing cannon and grappling hooks in preparation for our victim.

I looked back over the stern at our camp on the island. A handful of men stood in a group on the beach to guard the treasure we were about to divide, watching our progress. The mood on the boat was jubilant as most of the crew didn't care for the captain's decision to disband. But he had a troubled look on his face, as if some disaster was about to befall him that he stoically accepted. I finished coiling the line for the last grappling hook and went toward the captain. As first boy, it was my job to attend to his needs.

Gaspar called an order to turn out of the wind to allow the merchant leeway. We appeared to be the faster boat giving us the ability to choose our course for attack where the merchant vessel was fixed on its course, although there was no reason I could think that his sails were reefed. Judging the wind and the progress of the other boat, Gaspar called an order and we turned to port. The wind filled the sails and we picked up speed on what appeared to be a collision course with our prey. After taking the most favorable tack, there was nothing the other ship could do to avoid us. The energy running through the crew as they eagerly leaned over the rails and watched the gap close was one of the thrills of pirating and I couldn't help but be infected with it.

Our situation quickly changed as we approached. Just outside of our cannon range, the ship dropped the Union Jack and hoisted the stars and stripes of the American flag. We were powerless, our momentum too great to stop the boat as we watched the men on the deck of the other ship pull canvas covers from what appeared to be their cargo, revealing cannons. Someone yelled an order, we heard a loud boom and their ship rocked as the guns recoiled. A cloud of smoke formed above the frigate as the projectiles were launched and seconds later the destruction began. Mayhem took over as cannon balls and shrapnel fell around us, a destruction we had only witnessed as the aggressor and victor. The main mast came down after the second volley tearing a large portion of the gunwale away. I knew all was lost and it was every man for himself. We were in disarray, yet to fire even the small swivel cannon mounted on the rails.

Our ship was doomed and I looked down into the water at the men who had already lowered the boats and abandoned ship. Another broadside from the frigate sealed the fate of the Floridablanca and I jumped. The longboat capsized just as I landed on the deck throwing me into the cold Gulf water. I looked up and saw debris falling toward me from another hit and dove under water to avoid a falling sail that would surely drown me. My breath was almost gone when I finally surfaced and started swimming toward a piece of floating debris. The situation was dire for many of my mates, and I had no idea the fate of my captain, but I feared for his life as I had seen a figure holding a cutlass in one hand and the anchor chain in the other jump from the boat as the longboats from the frigate approached.

Bodies floated by as I kicked toward shore, not wanting to look back at the destruction. Downhearted about what I expected was Gaspar's fate, I knew enough that I was alive and although my survival was far from a sure thing right now, capture would result in a death by the rope. I kicked harder.

"Hurry, load the boats," I yelled at the men watching the devastation as I climbed out of the water, one through a spyglass, the others shielding their eyes from the sun. Several turned to me.

"What say Nick? Is the captain dead?" A man named Swift asked.

"All is lost. We have only minutes to load what we can and make for the mainland before the Navy comes for us." I turned to see if the pursuit had begun. Surely they knew of the island and the treasure it was rumored to contain. As soon as they had captured the remaining crew, they would come after us. I grabbed the spyglass from one of the men and put it to my eye. "Hurry. They'll check the water for survivors and this will be their next stop."

The men ran inland toward the ten chests stacked against a palm tree and started carrying them to the beach. I did some quick math in my head and ordered the men to put two chests in each boat. With ten men and five boats maybe we had a chance that at least some of us could escape. The water churned as we ran back and forth loading the chests in the boats. Once loaded we jumped in and reached for the oars. The paddle blades battled the water, one man on each side, as we pulled with all we had in the direction of the mainland.

My boat led the convoy and I pondered my new role as leader. No one had questioned me in our haste to escape the island.

Chapter Three

We made our way around the exposed seaward side of the island and were well into the protected waters of the sound when we paused. I looked across the large channel at the land on either side wondering where to go. A mile across the water in the direction of the mainland was the cover we sought. Dozens of small islands surrounded by shallow water were scattered along the coast. Exhausted, we knew we were in a life or death situation and we worked through the pain of our aching muscles, pulling hard on the oars. Thankfully we paddled with a flood tide, made even stronger by the full moon. If the tide had been outgoing, we would have been treading water, but instead the extra two knots helped push our boats toward land. Rhames sat by my side, grunting with every pull and giving me cross looks as his strokes, more powerful than mine kept moving the boat toward starboard where I sat. I knew the estuary as well as any man and navigated while he watched the horizon behind us for any sign of pursuit.

As we reached land, we collapsed on our oars, exhausted by the effort of the hour long row. We floated into a cove in the lee of a horseshoe-shaped island hidden from view from the seaward side. I had seen no boats yet, but we all knew they would come. The legend of the treasure on our boats was widespread, sought by both pirates and the United States Navy.

"Well Nick? What do you think?" Rhames said after he caught his breath.

I was shocked by the question. He was technically second in command after the captain, but most knew it was more for his loyalty and brutality than for his wits. My only guess was that after several years of bringing him orders from the captain, that he looked to me as his surrogate. I took the chance and retained the authority. Leaving our state of affairs to pirate law, meaning the consensus of the group, would probably result in several deaths and the loss of our treasure. When we were safe we could choose a leader, but for now I had an idea.

"They're bound to follow. I saw the captain go overboard with the anchor chain around his waist and his cutlass in his hand." The statement was met by murmurs of approval. Pirates lived hard and died young, with the exception of our captain who was sixty-five this year. I remembered the look on his face as we approached the disguised ship and thought he might have had second thoughts about retiring. Dying with your cutlass in your hand brought you to our version of Valhalla and those who fell in battle were revered. "I saw the ship go down, but there are no boats after us yet. We've got a good head start, but they'll be on our scent soon enough." I looked from man to man trying to gauge them from the looks on their faces. These were men, although equals by the code, who were used to taking orders.

I tried to anticipate the next move the Navy captain would make. The frigate would have put their longboats in the water as soon as the Floridablanca went down. I was guessing they had at least twenty boats - twice ours, each holding half a dozen well-armed men. The sun, although it was only a third way into the sky was near its winter zenith indicating noon. That would give us about five hours of daylight to reach a safe haven. Considering our head start and the tide change that would hamper their efforts this afternoon, I figured they would be no further than where we now sat by dusk.

"We've got to head inland." All eyes were on me and I heard my voice crack, belaying my nervousness. "The Peace River is at the end of the bay. There is a woman there that the captain trusted." I heard several ayes and the men readied to row. I looked over at Rhames and he nodded at me, a small smile on his face. Surely he knew that once we reached land he could overpower us and take the treasure for himself. There was not a man amongst us that would contest him - and he had the only pistol.

As we rowed through the small islands toward the point of land that marked the entrance to the Bay, I started to question my decision. My mouth was already dry and I realized we had no food or water. Fortunately, the December air was cooler and less humid than the summer months, but we would have to find drinking water by dark. The cover of the islands was behind us and we were exposed as we neared the headland. I looked past the point to the open water that lay beyond. Several times, the captain had taken me and several other men through here to a farm called Spanish Homestead where he favored the Lady Boggess. My plan was to reach the homestead and seek her sympathy and protection either through her hatred of the Navy for killing her husband or through bribery.

On our past trips to the farm, we had stopped for the night at a small village named Punta Gorda where I knew we could get food and water. To complicate matters, the near shore was totally exposed. We would have to row the two miles across open water to reach the southern shore and the small islands that would offer us protection. If we were to hug the north shore until dusk and then make the crossing, the landmass would hide the angle of approach of the pursuers. Once we reached the far shore we could use the cover of the islands and the full moon to reach Punta Gorda where several of us would sneak ashore and steal water and food. Thus provisioned, we could make for the mouth of the river and seek the aid of the captain's lady friend.

With nothing to do but pull on my oar I started to think ahead. Word would spread fast and the lure of the treasure we carried would bring out every bounty hunter in Florida. I also feared traveling overland through the territory; a war between the Americans and the Seminole Indians was brewing, making the land as dangerous as the ocean. The size and weight of the chests would necessitate a horse-drawn cart which was slow and noticeable. With only ten men to defend it, the treasure would be in jeopardy before we started. I looked back at the open water thinking it our best chance for escape.

Chapter Four

Wind blown spray flew over the bow of the boat as we pulled to our limits crashing through the waves in our path. We were soaked and despite the hard work, I was shivering. It was hard to tell how Rhames fared as he stared straight ahead and rowed. The waves were capped with white foam, some high enough to block our view of land when the boat fell into the trough. With the help of the outgoing tide, the crests stacked up in the entrance to the bay so close together they slammed the boat continuously. I chanced a glance at the other boats in our convoy when we crested a wave, and they were struggling as we were. At least to this point, we remained together.

With every glimpse of land, our situation looked worse. The island we were making for seemed to diminish in size. Was it possible the current was moving us backwards? I thought about asking Rhames, but his skill lay more with the pistol and cutlass than navigation. No, this was my call. I looked toward the sky for a sign and what I saw changed our course. A dark line of clouds was approaching. Not the huge puffy clouds with their dark anvil bottoms that wreaked havoc during the summer, but a long dark line etched across the horizon. There was no way to know how quickly it would hit us, but when it did, the wind would be fierce and would likely last for several days. All I knew was it was not visible several hours ago, meaning it was moving fast. We were in no way prepared for the rain and chill that accompanied these winter storms.

"Rhames," I yelled over the wind. He turned toward me. "We need to go back." I nodded my head toward the line of clouds that seemed even closer now.

"Aye," he replied and started to back his oar.

That was about as much as I could expect from him, but I needed to make sure the other boats knew our plan. I yelled at the top of my lungs, but the wind threw my words back in my face. Rhames must have noticed and yelled with me. His voice was lost as well. We had to signal the crews or the current would scatter us. I noticed the pistol stuck in his belt and yelled for him to fire. Without a word he withdrew the gun, pointed toward the sky and fired. The blast was deafening, and I turned to see if the other boats had heard. The sound had carried and heads turned. Now that we had their attention, I focused on the maneuver that was so simple in calm water, but dangerous with the present conditions.

I continued to pull forwards as Rhames back paddled, trying to time my strokes with his. The boat started to turn and I braced myself for the crux, when we would be beam on to the waves and in danger of capsizing. I closed my eyes and froze, not wanting to watch as we turned and the wave came over the boat.

"Row, dammit. Whatever happens - row harder," Rhames yelled.

I woke from my stupor and pulled as hard as I could. Finally the boat broke free from the friction of the water, but paused as if hanging on the wave. We were stalled, about to fall backwards and in danger of capsizing when we glanced at each other and with a furious attempt we both pulled at the same time. I pulled again, feeling only air and exhaled as we found ourselves on the crest of the wave. Having passed through the dangerous quarter the boat moved quickly toward the island we had just left.

We had done enough beach landings to know how to surf and despite being drenched and cold, the feeling of riding the waves was exhilarating. I looked back, a smile on my face that quickly disappeared when I saw the scene behind us. Two of the boats were following, another was struggling through the turn, but the last was gone, an oar floating in the water where the boat should have been. "Look," I yelled at Rhames and waited for him to turn.

I desperately searched for the men, but the only sign the boat had been there was the single oar. It was too loud with the wind blowing and waves crashing against the boat to hear anyone yell; if the men had survived, they were invisible in the white-capped water. Rhames, more pragmatic or less emotional than I, simply turned away and started to row again. He had been around long enough to know that there was nothing we could do to save the men, the boat or the treasure chests that were now on the bottom of the bay.

I felt a tinge of guilt as I looked away from the water, and focused on the land ahead. The captain had taught me how to use fixed points of land to determine a position on the water. It was easier with a compass, but I knew if I could find the right landmarks, that we could return in better conditions and recover the chests. We had sounded the entrance to the bay on previous trips and with the water only around ten feet where the boat went down, we could dive on the site. I struggled to line up any features that would be memorable.

My eyes went first to the headland on the left and I was able to line up two small islands that I knew. I scanned the coast to the right looking for another landmark. A tall palm leaning toward the water caught my eye and I searched the landscape behind it for anything that I could use to line it up and mark the position. I noticed a small mound behind the tree with a scrub oak and committed them to memory.

I'm not sure if Rhames knew what I was doing as he said nothing, but there was something about the look on his face that gave me the impression that he approved. With our mates lost, at least for now, the four boats stayed close, surfing the waves as we approached shore. The distance it had taken hours to row, we now covered in minutes and the waves settled as we moved behind one of the larger islands near the headland. I pointed toward an island and Rhames corrected his stroke change out course toward the small beach.

It was a relief to be back on land, but we were in dire trouble. We huddled on the beach shivering. There was no fresh water and we would be forced to forgo a fire to remain unseen. I looked around the island for anything that might be able to provide shelter for the coming storm.

Chapter Five

The rain pounding on the hull woke me and I wondered if it was daylight yet. At least the overturned boat kept us dry and with the eight of us huddled underneath it was warm, but I couldn't see outside. The wind howled and rain sheeted in as I raised an edge of the boat and looked out of our makeshift shelter. My stomach growled and my mouth was dry. The last thing I wanted to do was to leave the shelter, but we needed water badly.

I elbowed the man next to me and received a grunt and a jab back in return. "Swift. Get up. We need to get water."

"Boy. What do you want from me? I'm tired, lemme sleep."

I would not relent and pushed back, moving out of the way before he could reciprocate. "Now," I demanded pushing my authority as far as I dared. He rose and hit his head on the bottom of the boat, but helped me lift the edge enough so that we could crawl into the cold and wet night. It was a good blow, the line of clouds we had seen earlier were surely upon us. I looked around for anything that would contain rainwater, but found little. There was water in the boats, but it was dirty and mixed with salt water. We needed fresh clean water.

"Dig a hole," I called to Swift over the wind.

I didn't wait for an answer, but went straight to a small palm tree nearby and started pulling the broad leaves off. The palm was more a bush than the large coconut palms that towered overhead and the leaves were wide and solid. I took a handful and set them down next to the hole that Swift was digging and went back for more. When I returned he had excavated a three foot by three foot hole about a foot deep in the sand. I started to line the bottom with the palm leaves overlapping them to prevent leakage. Swift caught on and started another hole a few feet away. My hole was just about finished now and the water was already about an inch deep in the bottom. I kneeled down and with cupped hands pulled water from the hole and drank. Swift came up alongside and did the same. We drank greedily from the hole, the fresh rainwater soothing our dry throats and he gave me a reassuring nod.

Finally sated, I looked at the sea in the direction of our island and noticed the fires. Despite the rain, the Navy was burning our shelters probably out of frustration; the weather keeping them from following. Swift saw it too and nodded at me. As uncomfortable as we were, the storm was protecting us from the hangman's noose.

Fifteen minutes later, we crawled back under the boat and shivered in the darkness, but at least we would have water. I was too wet and cold to sleep anymore so I waited out the hours before dawn planning our next action. They would surely come after us in the morning. These kinds of storms lasted several hours, not days. The wind might blow, but it wouldn't stop them - not with pirates to hang and treasure to recover. We would need an early start and a long row to reach the homestead by nightfall so I waited for the first sign of dawn and woke the men.

"Get up. We've got to move," I waited a minute for them to gather their wits. "They've burned the island and now they're after us." They started moving quickly now, knowing the consequences if we were caught. We flipped the boat we had used for shelter and pushed it to the edge of the water alongside the other boats. I pointed out the wells we had dug and they ran over and started drinking. We had no vessels to take water with us so I implored them to drink their fill as I scanned the horizon for any pursuit. Fires were still burning on the island and I could see the long boats rowing for the frigate. They would be aboard and be under sail in minutes. If I had to guess they would move into the mouth of the harbor and dispatch the boats from there rather than have them cross the sound as we had.

"Hurry up. Drink and let's go." I grabbed several of the men and started tipping the other boats over to remove the water accumulated overnight. The rain had stopped, but the wind stayed strong. I could only hope the tide would be our ally as each man drank again and we pushed the boats off the beach.

The wind remained from the north and at our backs. This time, with a favorable wind and a slack tide, we were able to cover the water it had taken us hours yesterday in less than half that. We faced the island we had camped on as we rowed. I looked over my shoulder fixed on an island ahead to correct course, but when I faced backwards as is the normal position to row, I lined up the landmarks I had committed to memory yesterday marking where the boat had sunk and further etched them in my mind. The water was too dark to see the bottom as we passed the spot and I said a silent prayer for the men we had lost. My focus turned to the maze of small islands ahead of us. I tapped Rhames on the shoulder, pointed to the small cay I was aiming for and he adjusted his pull to change our course. Another half hour of hard rowing and we pulled behind the small island which screened us from our pursuers.

Through a small opening in the brush we could see that the frigate was now anchored outside of the Boca Grande pass, in the mouth of the channel. The large vessel could go no farther without the time consuming practice of dropping a lead every few feet. Longboats were dropping from its side and we could see men climbing down the cargo netting to the boats. Several were already fully manned waiting in the water. I looked around at the men as they looked at me and could see the indecision on their faces.

We had no time to waste. The Navy boats were bigger, and manned by six to eight men each. With that many oars in the water they could easily catch us. We would have to rely on stealth to escape the faster boats.

Chapter Six

I was counting on my knowledge of the area to lose the Navy boats. In the months we had holed up here, I had been in the marshy backcountry many times, foraging for oysters and netting fish between the narrow shoals. We had no chance of outrunning the larger, better manned boats that followed; our best chance was to ditch the boats and head inland, but then the treasure would weigh us down.

We brought the boats together in the lee of the island and I found all eyes on me.

"Alright, Nick," Rhames said. "What's the plan?"

I hesitated, still uncomfortable with my authority and unsure if the men had the fortitude for the dangers that lay ahead. "We can't lose them on the open water. There are too many. Their boats are faster and they're well-armed." I started to plead my case and waited while the men looked at each other and grunted in assent. "I'm thinking we row down the coast and hide out."

"That's a lot of open water to cover," one of the men named Red said as he slapped the side of his boat. Several other men nodded in agreement.

"We'll have to row at night, but if we stay out here, we're dead men and all this will be lost," I waved my hands at the chests.

"What about the lady?" another asked.

"That's the first place they'll look," I responded.

Rhames eyed the group instantly stopping the dissent. "Boy's right."

That was all he said, but it was all that was needed. In agreement we turned to the West and led the small convoy through the chain of islands. By noon, the wind had started to die and the rowing became easier, but as our anxiety about the seas diminished our hunger and thirst began to dominate our thoughts. "We have to find some food," I said to Rhames who only grunted.

"We get a turtle, it'll hold us for a while." I pointed toward an inlet that looked like it turned into a small river. "They won't think of looking in there and I have an idea."

He pulled hard on his oar and we swung toward the mouth of the inlet. The other boats followed and we made landfall on a gravel beach about a hundred feet in. We gathered around the boats, the group again looking to me for leadership.

"They're going to think that we are heading for the Spanish Homestead and the Lady Boggess. We should be safe in here. Red, take five men and follow the river in. We need fresh water and food - oysters, turtle - even a gator. Some coconuts would be good as well.

"What about you?" Red asked. "You gonna sit here and sleep?"

I met the first resistance to my leadership easily. "Rhames and I are going to create a diversion." They all looked at me again. "We need to empty one of the chests." They eyed me suspiciously but I ignored them. "We meet back here at sunset - and be ready to row."

"What about the loot?" Red asked.

He was quickly becoming my opposition, "We empty one chest and combine its contents with the others. You take the rest." That seemed to satisfy him and we split into two groups. Rhames and I waited as the men took three of the boats and started to move inland. We set the empty chest in the boat so it was visible above the gunwales.

"Well, I hope you have a plan." Rhames said.

I sat on the beach with my back to the boat. "We need the tide." I said and closed my eyes to give the illusion that I actually knew what I was doing. Unable to sleep, my mind was trying to finish cooking the half-baked plan that I had sold the men on. I was counting on the tide to float the empty boat toward the Peace River, giving the Navy men reinforcement for what they already thought; that we were heading to Spanish Harbor. We would hike back here after sending the boat. With their attention upriver, I intended to regroup at sunset and head west using the night for cover. The chain of islands that protected us ended a mile from here and we would be exposed for several hours once we left their cover and visible to the frigate until we reached the channel leading to the Caloosahatchee River. From there we could continue down the coast and seek refuge in the marshes.

We would need to leave close to midnight and before the moon rose. We would pass the river mouth, exit the protection of the waterway and head for Estero Bay. The portage required to enter the bay from the North ought to discourage pursuit. The bay offered excellent vantage points to observe anyone entering from sea and its many islands offered refuge. We could regroup and plan there. Rhames was asleep when I woke him an hour later. "Time." He seemed to like simple commands.

He rose and shook his dreadlocks out. With his help, we pushed the boat into the shallow water. We jumped into the lead boat and started to row, the empty hull with its barren chest followed behind. The wind had died a bit, but was still brisk and helped push us toward the mouth of the Peace River as we exited the protection of the inlet. I motioned for Rhames to hold water. The wind and tide were working in our favor now. We stayed in the lee of the islands and out of view of the long boats I expected to be close by. At the headland we beached the boat. As I was about to push the sacrificial craft into the current, Rhames stopped me. "It's a bit of a walk back there."

I nodded and we pushed the boat off the bank. We stood there as the tide and wind took it around the headland and into the river. I heard someone yell and turned to look back into the bay where a handful of longboats were speeding toward the river mouth. The boat had been spotted. With no time to watch our plan unfold, we started a fast hike back toward the inlet, trudging through the marshy muck that permeated the shallows. As we approached, I saw a small stream of smoke coming from the beach we had departed from and picked up our pace.

Chapter Seven

"Douse it now!" I yelled as we pushed through the brush and onto the beach. Rhames didn't wait, he ran to the fire pit and hurled sand onto the flames. The men had killed and brought back a large loggerhead turtle which now lay on its back in the embers. Worried we might have been spotted, I sent two men with one of the boats to the mouth of the inlet to stand watch. The Navy ship lay less than a half-mile away and although we were screened by the island and brush they could still see the smoke.

The fire was smoldering now and we pulled the turtle out. "You want to eat now, it needs to be raw. Open up the belly and start butchering. We'll take it with us, maybe get a hot meal tomorrow, but before that we have a long night ahead." Several men pulled knives from their belts and I flinched for a second, thinking they were coming for me, but they went to work on the turtle. They sliced the belly and started cutting slabs of meat from the two hundred fifty pound animal. This would be enough food to see us for a week, if we were careful and able to preserve it. Within minutes all the meat was out of the shell, sitting on palm fronds cut from the brush. "Clean the shell too. We'll need that."

I caught a look from Rhames and followed him down the beach.

"You're doing well, boy. They listen to you and what you say makes sense," he paused and pulled on his braided beard. "You take the lead, but watch me."

This was the most I had ever heard him speak. I grasped his meaning, and thought we could make a good team. He had let me know that I could lead, but he was in charge. I could live with this arrangement; it would keep me alive. Without Rhames behind me, the other men would soon turn against each other. With his menacing figure backing me up, the crew would fall in line. Red seemed to be the only dissenter among them and I knew from the past few years how he worked. He would whisper to the men, planting the seeds for unrest, then sit back and wait for them to blossom. We walked back to the makeshift camp.

I looked up at the sun, which was starting to sink in its low winter arc. I had planned on pushing off around midnight when the watches on the Navy boat would be less attentive. We had a long exposed row before we reached the cover of Pine Island and the protection of the clusters of islands along the shore and a good part of the journey would be in clear sight of the frigate anchored in the mouth of the harbor. I sent a relief party to replace the men on watch and lay back in the sand. Some of the men were eating raw turtle, but though my stomach rumbled, I was not ready for raw meat. If all went to plan, we would be far enough up the river by tomorrow morning to start a fire and smoke the meat. Small bands of Indians were common along the river and our fire would blend with theirs.

I tried to sleep, but between the cotton in my mouth, the rumble in my stomach, and my thoughts racing through my mind, I failed. Although we had a good chance of escaping detection and reaching the bay below the mouth of the river, we were far from safe. The diversion would have been discovered by now and the long boats were probably on their way back to the frigate. I had no doubt the captain of the Navy ship would send more boats, but he would wait until morning, giving us a decent head start.

Rhames came and sat by me, "Don't take a watch, not something the captain would do. Better to stay here and keep an eye on these worthless bastards."

I nodded. "We need to leave around midnight. That'll give us six hours to get past the mouth of the river. I'm guessing it close to twenty miles. You think the men have it in them?"

"They've got the treasure - they'll die for it."

He was right and that brought up my next conundrum. We were running heavy; the chests loaded and cumbersome. The smart thing to do would be to bury them here on the beach and travel light to escape. We could double back when we knew our pursuers had given up and split the bounty. But I could already see the looks cast back and forth at the chests and knew the greed of the men. There was no chance any of them would let the treasure out of their sight. Trust among pirates was rare if it even existed at all.

The time passed slowly. I changed the watch one more time and tried to rest. As the sky darkened, I started to second guess my decision. Confident that the diversion had been discovered by now, maybe doubling back and going toward the Peace River was the safer route. Would the Navy captain be shrewd enough to think us patient enough to wait them out and follow our own diversion? Pirates, by nature, were impatient and I tried to place myself in his place, asking myself what I would do. My answer surprised me and I knew the Peace River was the wrong destination. Even if the Navy searched elsewhere, the river was heavily populated and word would surely have reached the settlers there. Everyone would have an eye out for us and the treasure. The men were all restless and I decided to scout the mouth of the river and if all was clear we would move now.

Chapter Eight

With my first power struggle behind me, I still felt oddly self-conscious leading. I would stay in command, but Rhames had made it clear that he would have veto power and would back me as long as he agreed. The politics would wait; at this point I was focused on escaping the Navy and keeping the group intact. Getting the men safe, fed and watered was a top priority. It was hard to control a hungry group, and as I had learned yesterday there were some willing to risk their lives and the treasure for a hot meal. It would be a constant battle to fight their need for immediate gratification. We needed to get off the water by late afternoon, somewhere safe where we could make a fire.

It turned out to be an easy row, the elements all in our favor. We stayed quiet during the night, not knowing if there were any Navy scouts on the water or boat crews camped nearby. I thought they had gone after our decoy boats, but a shrewd captain would have sent boats toward Pine Island as well. It was a misty cold night and we were thankful when the sun rose. We had reached our goal for the night and the landmass blocked the frigate's view of us. Protected again by the islands near shore, the men's spirits picked up with the sun and as the morning wore on, we rowed through Buzzards Bay with no sign of the Navy men. As we exited the bay, I estimated we were half way down Pine Island and started thinking where we could camp for the night. It was essential that we could find a camp with fresh water and where we could start a fire. I knew I would start losing the confidence of the men if we continued in this condition.

"We need to cross to the island and camp," I told Rhames, the first words we had spoken all night.

"Aye," he responded.

Ahead of us was a large island in the center of the channel. We changed course toward the back side, further screening us from any pursuit. As we reached Pine Island, I started looking for a place to camp, but the coast was marshy and looked less than hospitable. From my position facing backwards as I rowed, I could see the faces of the men in the boats behind us and knew we would have to make camp soon. Around a bend, I pointed toward a small inlet. For better or worse this was it. The adrenaline I was running on for the last two days was waning and the men had reached their breaking point.

"Is this it then?" someone called from another boat.

I tried to exude confidence and replied, "It is." Just as I said it, we lurched forward as the bottom of the boat scraped an oyster bar and our oars smashed against the barnacles grounding us in the entrance. I jumped out and started to push, hoping it would look like I knew the obstacle was there and it was all part of the plan. Again, Rhames sensed my predicament and jumped out. The boat floated across the bar easily without our weight and we guided it over the shoal through the calf deep water. On the other side of the obstruction we hopped back in and continued rowing, watching behind us as the other boats followed our lead.

Two more bends came in quick succession and I started looking for a place to land. The marshes soon turned into gravel beaches and

I nodded my head toward one. We beached the boats, got out and stretched the stiffness from our joints. The land under my feet felt good, although my legs were wobbly after nearly eight hours in the boat. The other boats grounded and we pulled them above the high tide line. We milled around, exploring the immediate area, not knowing where to start. The island was nowhere near as hospitable as Gasparilla Island. Mosquitos swarmed and every step needed to be guarded less you step into a marshy pit.

"Let's start a fire. It's daylight. If we use dry wood it won't smoke badly." Several men moved toward a mound and started to dig out a fire pit while others moved inland to scrounge for wood. Twenty minutes later, Rhames struck his flint and the coconut husks caught. Soon the wood above was crackling and I looked to the sky, happy the smoke was almost invisible. We were used to camp life, and there were no orders needed as we sorted ourselves out, everyone performing the tasks best suited for them. The meat was smoking over the fire now and I went to the beach and pushed a boat into the water.

"Oysters," I yelled as I caught the looks of several of the men thinking that I was absconding with the treasure chests onboard. I rowed to the bar at the inlet, both to collect the mollusks and more importantly to check if any boats were near. Thankful we were still unnoticed, I hopped out of the boat and started harvesting oysters, prying them off with my knife. I had a large pile in the bottom of the boat when I pulled off the bar and started back to camp. On the beach, the men were gathered around the fire, eating turtle and drinking the succulent juice from the coconuts they had foraged. It seemed, at least for tonight we were safe.

Several of the men talked amongst themselves and I was surprised I had no interest in their conversation. I started to appreciate the value of Rhames as I fought sleep and finished cooking the meat and oysters. The fire would have to be extinguished before dusk and it would be another cold night, but we had warm food in our bellies and our thirst was sated from the coconut water.

Everyone was asleep now and I stood to walk the camp, keeping the first watch and sorting out our provisions in case we needed to make a hasty exit. I split the meat, wrapping it in palm fronds to keep the bugs off. We were into December and it was dryer and less buggy than the summer months, but this was Florida, and there were always bugs. I gathered ripe coconuts, fallen from the wind the other night and set a dozen in each boat as well. Finally after what I thought was four hours, I woke another man and laid down in one of the boats to rest.

Chapter Nine

The unmistakable sound of steel striking steel and the grunts of men woke me. I looked around trying to get my bearings and found the clearing crowded with men fighting at close quarters.

I left the cover of the boat and crept toward Rhames who stuck his pistol in my hand. "Guard the treasure," he said and ran to the fight.

I went to the boats, the chests still loaded where we had left them and started pacing back and forth. There was no immediate threat to me or the boats, at least not yet, and I was able to observe what was happening. We were fighting a group of men, maybe a half dozen all dressed as we were. I looked at the gravel beach, not seeing a boat, and wondered who they were and how they had gotten here. The most dangerous unknown was if there were reinforcements on the way, but at least I knew from the ragtag dress of the men it wasn't the Navy.

They must have come overland, probably from the channel which ran between the barrier islands and our location. I heard a man scream in what sounded like Cajun and I started to piece together what was going on. Jean Laffite and some of his crew had escaped

Galveston earlier this year, running from the same Navy that now sought us. They had set up a small camp on an island south of ours and he and our captain, both aging and wishing to retire, had become friends often talking about joining forces and heading to Columbia where they might obtain Naval commissions and live out their years. They must have seen our ship go down and after seeing the Navy burn our village had joined the pursuit. It was no secret some of our men had sought out Laffite to join his crew when we disbanded. They knew we had treasure and were greedy for it.

More men came through the brush and it looked like we would be overwhelmed, but Rhames saw them and rallied our men. We stood a better chance to escape if we scuttled one of our boats so with one eye toward the fight, I started to load the provisions I had split last night into two boats. Just as I finished, Rhames cut through several intruders and fought his way toward me, yelling at the men to follow. Laffite's men, guessing our motive started to pursue. I took the pistol and fired at their group. This stopped them momentarily and allowed our men to reach the boats. Rhames ordered several of the men into a semi-circle to protect us.

"Get the treasure in two the boats and trash the other." I yelled over the fracas. Understanding that our only means of escape was by water. A few men fell back from the fight, flipped the empty boat and started to punch holes in the bottom with rocks. Rhames and I moved the chests to the two remaining boats and we pushed them into the water. "Fall back!" I ordered and the men jumped in the boats and manned the oars. We looked at the others staring at our escape, now knee deep in the water and unable to follow.

Rhames handed me the black powder. The flintlock pistol reloaded and the pan primed, I got another shot off and reloaded again. When I looked up ready to fire, they were out of range. More than a dozen men stood on the beach waving cutlasses at us as we made our escape. But off to the side, I noticed what looked like one of our men held at knife point by two of the intruders. I counted the men in the boats and confirmed my sighting. My short reign as leader was faltering. In two days I had lost three men, three boats and two treasure chests.

The only way out of the estuary was over the oyster bar where we grounded yesterday, but the tide was high and even with the heavily-laden boats we just scraped the hulls as we floated over. I moved toward the bow, shielding my eyes from the rising sun as I looked for any other boats. The Navy frigate was probably still anchored at the mouth of the harbor, about to start the search afresh with the new day. This time I suspected they would send boats in this direction as well. The unknown was Laffite. If the old pirate had seen or heard the fate of the Floridablanca, he would guess the Navy frigate was anchored to the North and move his ships to block the Southern exit from the sound. He would then send out small parties like the one we encountered to search where the Navy was not yet looking. The two exits blocked we had no choice but to abandon my plan to seek refuge in Estero Bay and make for the river. The Caloosahatchee was dangerous and unknown country, it source rumored to be a massive inland lake that had a river of grass running south into the Florida Keys. If we made it to the Keys, we could figure it out from there.

"To port," I yelled to the men who had their backs to the bow. We crossed the channel and made for the mouth of the river. Just as we reached open water, I saw Laffite's boat anchored where I expected it. We were too small for him to see from that distance and I ordered the rowers into a small inlet. Not knowing if it had an exit or not we blindly rowed south hoping it was fed from the river. I had no idea if we could make the river from here without a portage, but we needed a place to hole up and regroup. I looked back toward the rowers and it was then that I saw the blood mixing with the water in the bottom of the boat.

"Which one of you is hurt?" I asked looking at the backs of the two men.

"Aye, but it nothing," Rhames responded.

It didn't look like nothing from the amount of blood mixing with the seawater in the boat and I looked for a place to land. If something happened to Rhames, I had no doubt my short tenure as leader would be over. I directed the boats toward the only dry land I saw, a small beach. I jumped out and pulled the boat onto the beach wanting to go to Rhames right away, but also aware that would look like a sign of weakness. Instead I waited for the men to disembark and scatter on the beach before I went to him.

The cut was long and deep across his stomach. If there were a surgeon amongst us he surely would have stitched the wound and if we had supplies I would have attempted the same. Instead I took off my shirt and tore several strips from the tail, helped him remove his shirt and checked the cut. It looked clean and I bound the linen around his body hoping to stem the blood flow. He lay down, his face pale from blood loss and exertion and I looked at the other men wondering what they were thinking.

Chapter Ten

We stood in a circle and I watched each man as their eyes moved from Rhames, to the chests and finally to me. It was an uneasy feeling standing there being scrutinized and I put on my stone face. I couldn't afford one uneasy look or gesture. Rhames lay in the boat, moaning in pain. There was nothing more I could do for him - time would tell if he was to survive. My problem now was to keep the crew rallied around me.

"Red," I looked at their leader. "We should scout the river mouth. We can't stay here too long." I looked around. There was no freshwater and starting a fire here would be out of the question. Although sheltered by the estuary, the smoke from the smallest fire would be seen by the watching eyes of the Navy and Lafitte. Without waiting for an answer I looked at each of the men, fixing my gaze on them until they made eye contact. "You men stay here and keep an eye on him," I pointed to Rhames, who was trying to sit upright. "No fires and keep a watch. We are nowhere close to safe."

"You heard the man," Red said as he picked up his cutlass and started walking away, "You coming?" he looked at me.

I took one look at Rhames who nodded to me in assurance. He was clearly in pain, but was sitting upright in the stern of the boat now, the flintlock pistol secure in his belt.

He removed the gun and handed it to me. "Go," he said.

I slid the barrel into my waistband and went after Red who was already a few hundred feet away. When I caught him, he looked at me with a half-smile that concealed his intentions. The smile turned to a frown when he saw the weapon in my possession. Rhames may have saved himself as well as me by giving me the pistol. If he had passed out with the gun, one of the men would surely have shot him, and with the weapon I held the upper hand with Red.

We trudged along the bank, fighting through the calf-deep muck along the mangrove-lined shores. Although the temperature was fair, within minutes we were sweating from the exertion of walking through mud.

"How far you reckon, Mister Nick?"

We had been moving for what I figured was half an hour. I stopped to catch my breath and looked behind us. If we had gone a mile, it would have been hopeful. I had never been in the estuary before, but from where its entry lined up with the tip of the island to seaward, I estimated we had to cover two miles to reach the river mouth. "About the same. Maybe another mile," I replied and started moving again. Sweat stung my eyes and my throat was parched, but this was not the time to show weakness.

We picked up our pace as we heard the grunts from several gators concealed in a small creek on our left. Finally the bottom started to turn hard and we could see the river. Although it was a relief to be able to walk on hard bottom, I noticed the water was getting shallower as well. By the time we reached the middle of the small pass, we were ankle deep at best. The mangrove roots along the shore revealed what I suspected, that we were close to high tide now. If we wanted to use this pass, and we had little choice as any other route would expose us, we would have to portage the boats. Red must have come to the same conclusion.

"Gonna be a bit of work here to get the boats over," he said and turned around to go back.

"Wait. I want to go out to the point and have a look."

"Suit yourself," he said and remained where he was.

I ran the hundred yards to the seaward side of the small inlet and went down the beach as far as I dared. I didn't want him out of my sight and turned back several times to confirm he was still there. From the point, I had an unobstructed view of the river mouth and as I suspected, Lafitte's frigate guarded the entrance, but the shoals near shore forced him to stand half a mile out to sea. I couldn't see any long boats in the water, but I suspected he would launch a reconnaissance before the day was out. Our only chance would be to make the portage and enter the river at night.

Lafitte was a seasoned and capable seaman. He and his men had been double-crossed by the US government following his help in fighting the British in their attack on New Orleans in the war of 1812. The Navy soon labeled his small community on an island near Galveston a pirate haven and burned it to the ground. I considered myself fortunate to meet the man and had learned much about both strategy and business by listening to his talks with Gasparilla. They had become friends, but there was no doubt Lafitte knew of his demise and now sought the treasure.

I ran back to Red who stood in the same spot.

"Well?"

"Lafitte's ship is in the mouth of the river. We're going to need to make the portage tonight if we want to get upriver."

"There's no other way," Red stated.

"No. The Navy is on the other end and Lafitte is here. Neither will be willing to go too far upriver, especially if they don't have any reason to suspect we have gone there."

"Let's get back then," Red said and started wading through the muck.

We reached the clearing an hour later and collapsed by the boats. Rhames was still alive, but hovering on the edge of consciousness. I looked toward the west to gauge how much daylight was left and realized we would have several hours to wait before leaving. "We move in two hours," I called to the men and went for one of the boats where several coconuts were floating in the bilge water. I took two and went toward Rhames who opened one eye. From my belt, I pulled out a small dagger, took the steel point and inserted it into the coconut. Once it was embedded I started to push and twist. It was far from clean, but I pulled the blade out and saw a residue of milk on it. I handed it to Rhames and watched with satisfaction as he held it to his mouth and drained the juice. I took the other and repeated the process, keeping this one for myself, before cleaving them open and sharing the meat.

Rhames looked better after the nourishment, but I was worried about his wound and knew I needed to care for it while we still had daylight. I went to him and started to remove the dressing. The bleeding had stopped, but the wound was weeping and ugly. Its edges looked like the leaves of a palmetto palm and were starting to turn green and fill with puss. I left him and went to gather the discarded coconut halves and brought several back. From these I scooped the paste from the edges and started to apply it to the wound. He jumped when I touched it, but knew as I did that something in the oily meat of the coconut helped the healing process. I just hoped he wasn't too far gone.

I left the wound open to look for anything that might help me close it and went back to the men who were huddled together talking. They stopped as soon as I approached and I knew something was amiss. As I turned to go back toward Rhames, one of the men jumped on my back. He held me while another slammed his fist into my stomach. I doubled over in pain. Without knowing I reached for the gun, heard it fire and collapsed onto the sand, thinking I had shot myself. As I hit the ground I realized it wasn't me, but the man holding me. The other men stood frozen staring at me, the smoking pistol still in my hand.

Chapter Eleven

As quickly as I could, I reloaded, watching the process with one eye while my other watched the men gathered around the downed man. Their disorganization gave me time to finish loading before they could act and I regained an advantage as I held the pistol in my hand.

"Do we have a problem here?" I asked looking at Red who stared at the ground. I met the eyes of the other three dissenters one at a time.

None spoke, but slowly they met my gaze having realized their gambit had failed. We were six men now with two boats, barely enough man power to move the chests. I looked back at Red, "We together or not? If we stay together we can do this."

Red nodded and looked at his compatriots. They seemed to reach an unspoken agreement. "Sorry about that Mister Nick," he shrugged. "Our greed got the best of us."

"I want a vote right now. I'm either captain or we elect someone else," I said. It was a gamble, but the pistol in my hand gave me courage. Red was the decision maker for the other three and I appealed to him, "We need the numbers to stay alive and keep the treasure."

"You seem to have learned a bit from the captain." Everyone dropped their heads at the mention of Gasparilla. "But all the same, we can split the loot and go our separate ways. With just you, and Rhames near dead, I don't expect you'd get far."

He was right and I looked down in defeat.

From behind me I heard a rough voice, "You'd all be best to listen and acknowledge your captain. I know you bastards and not one of you will be alive in a day without him."

Red finally broke the silence, "Let's hear your plan then. Then we'll vote."

I paused knowing what I had in mind was the hard way, but I didn't want to sugarcoat anything and be forced to have a daily mutiny to deal with. "We can't go to sea. Lafitte's at the mouth of the river and he has Rudy, who's probably sworn him allegiance and told him who we are as well as how we are provisioned and armed. On the other side is the Navy." I looked at the men who were focused on me now and paused, "And none of us wants to be caught by them." If we were caught by Lafitte, we stood a better than average chance of surviving by joining his band. The Navy on the other hand would hang us.

I could tell from their looks that I had them and let the silence linger for a moment before I continued. "There is another way. There're no maps and it'll be a long and dangerous path, but the Indians say the river empties into a huge lake whose southern end turns into a river of grass that leads to the Keys. They won't expect us to take that route."

I tried to look uninterested, but strained to listen as the men gathered in a circle. A minute later they faced me again.

Red spoke for the group, "Aye, Nick. It's the only plan. You've got our votes."

I wasted no time trying to act like I expected this outcome. "Get some food in you and rest for an hour. Then we're off." I turned and went to attend to Rhames.

"Nicely done," he said.

"I'd be dead without you."

"Stop that and get me some food. I don't expect you to carry me through this."

I looked at him and focused on the wound. I'd have to find a way to stitch it if he was to travel. The way it looked now, one wrong movement and he would spill his guts. I looked around and grabbed a discarded coconut husk. Carefully I started to peel the fibers, called coir into foot-long segments and laid them next to Rhames. Now I needed a needle. I got up and moved toward the men who were eating turtle meat and drinking from coconuts. They sat in a circle as far from the dead man as the clearing allowed. There were several pieces of meat laid out and I took two and brought one to Rhames while I chewed the other.

The meat gave me an idea, and I went to the shell laying in one of the boats. With my dagger I sliced a sliver off the edge of the shell about three inches long and went back to Rhames. I ate and whittled, fashioning a crude needle from the shell. With the fiber threaded I looked at him.

"Get some help to hold me and get on with it," he said as he finished the meat.

I got up and went to the men, explained my plan and waited as they finished eating and followed me back to where Rhames lay. One of the men gave him his dagger and Rhames put the wooden handle in his mouth and nodded. The men held him tightly as I prepared to suture the wound. The needle met resistance, the skin tougher than I had anticipated. He screamed and stared at me with bulging eyes as I forced it through. It took several stitches to get a feel for it but I slowly closed the wound. Finished, I looked up and saw him still conscious, his teeth firmly in the wood handle of the dagger and drool running from his mouth. I removed the dagger and he relaxed. After a few deep breaths I recoated the wound with coconut oil and tore another strip from my shirt to bind it. Satisfied I had done all I could, I laid down exhausted.

***

An hour later we were loaded and started to move out, three to a boat. For the first time Rhames and I were separated, but this was my decision. Only two could row the boats and he was incapable and I was the weakest. The water was calm and we reached the beach by the spot we would portage at dusk. I got out of the boat and went to scout the river mouth when suddenly I heard a large explosion. It was almost dark now and I ran toward the point where a glow from a fire showed in the distance. The outline of two ships were visible where only Lafitte's was earlier. The Navy frigate fired again.

I ran back to the beach. "The Navy just fired on Lafitte. This is our chance." I started pulling a boat across the sand. The men quickly ran to the boats and followed my lead. I had planned on waiting until later that night, when there was less chance of being spotted, but the Navy had given us our opportunity. Anyone not on the two ships would be watching the action and not the river mouth.

After five minutes of back-breaking work, the boats floated in the knee-deep water and we hopped in. The men took to the oars and pulled into the river. From my position in the bow I was able to look backwards at the fire blazing as Lafitte's ship went down.

EPISODES 1-4
TIDES of FORTUNE
STEVEN BECKER
1 ESCAPE
2 The BIG LAKE
3 RIVER of GRASS
4 CAYO HUESO

Sign up for my newsletter

Click or enter the address below

Get Wood's Ledge for FREE!

mactravisbooks.com

While tarpon fishing in the backcountry of the Florida Keys, Mac Travis discovers a plot to drill for oil in the pristine waters.

After his life is threatened he teams up with his long time friend and mentor, Wood, to uncover a plot that leads to the top echelons of power in Washington DC. An action packed short story featuring underwater and boating scenes

TIDES OF FORTUNE

episode two

STEVEN BECKER

Chapter One

The pre-dawn mosquitos swarmed around my head as I peered through the bushes and observed the activity in the camp. The women were out raking the coals to restart their fire. The dim outlines turned to identifiable figures as the sun rose and filtered through the scrub oaks. We needed to know if this band of Indians would be hostile or approachable. The coastal tribes were friendly and traded with us, but we had heard stories of the Indians further inland - tales of cannibalism and savagery We had covered many miles since we had entered the river, and it was hard to believe it had only been a day since we had seen Lafitte's ship sunk by the Navy. With three in each boat, we were able to rotate rowers and sleep in turns allowing us to continue non-stop, and I estimated we had covered half the distance to the big lake. During the night, we had passed several small Indian villages and I hoped they either hadn't seen us or would keep quiet about our passing.

Relations with the Indians were tense as of late. The peaceful Calusa and Tequesta tribes had merged with the Crow, forced to move south by Andrew Jackson and the United States Army. They called themselves the Seminoles and were wary of white men. This was the largest village we had passed, and I made sure to put some distance between us before we found a beach upriver to make camp. The river had changed through the course of our paddle, from the more tropical coast cluttered with palms to the cypress, scrub oaks and brush that now surrounded us. The ground was still sandy, but more like dirt than the coastal sand we were used to. Along with the change in flora, the fauna had changed as well. Alligators were still around, and deer were often visible drinking along the shore. Panthers were rumored to be in these woods and I was sure I had heard the roar of a big cat, although I had not seen it.

My concern was that our boats were no longer suitable for the shallow and winding river. Since late last night, the water had become riddled with shoals, and our boats had grounded several times. I knew the Indians used canoes, lighter and more maneuverable craft made from burned out cypress logs than the heavy oak longboats we had. If we were to continue to the big lake and then south through the river of grass, we would need several of these vessels to carry us and the treasure. The hollowed-out cypress logs we had seen the natives fish from, in the estuaries along the coast were perfect for navigating these waters. With no time to make them ourselves, the only option was to steal them. I hoped as I watched the camp wake up and start their daily routines that this tribe would docile and an easy target.

Swift stirred next to me, "What are we looking for anyway?"

I moved closer to whisper, "I'm not sure. We need to gauge the fight in them. Just watch."

It was fully light out and the sun was warming the clearing. We had been eating both raw and smoked turtle for days and my mouth salivated as the smell of food cooking over the fire was blown in our direction by the light breeze. I had picked this spot to observe from because it was downwind; as there were tales that some of their men could smell like a deer. That decision was causing me the discomfort of not only the smoke but also reminding me of my hunger. I could tell it was affecting Swift as well and I extended my arm placing it on his shoulder to calm him.

The native men were up and about now, strutting around the camp shirtless, wearing only breechcloths and moccasins, their heads shaved with only a section of hair remaining down the middle of their scalp. They were gathering bows and spears, looking like they were about to go hunting. If they went overland, we could steal several of their boats and be long gone before they discovered the theft, but if they took the boats we would have to move on. I had already realized that although the treasure we carried could buy whatever we needed, showing it would lead to certain trouble. Whoever received our bounty would surely use it to trade near the coast and questions would be asked. The loot needed to stay intact until we reached somewhere that it would not attract attention. That place by my reckoning was Cayo Hueso, the last island in the string of cays flowing from the end of the peninsula.

The native men were moving out, and Swift stirred, but I grabbed his shoulder, this time with more pressure. I thought we were discovered and tensed as they moved toward us. I squeezed Swift harder and relaxed as they passed us on an adjacent trail. There were only a few older men left along with the women and children in the clearing. I waited several minutes to make sure the men were gone and started to rise when I saw her.

She was taller than the rest of the women by several inches, but it was the blue eyes that separated her from them. Her hair, once blonde, still showed some hints of the straw color through the dirt. I stared across the clearing at Rory and knew the task of getting out with a few boats had just become more difficult. The girl who I figured to be about my age had been taken by Gasparilla along with her mother in a raid about a year ago. She had been kept with the other women awaiting either ransom or the whims of the captain on

Captiva Island. In my role as cabin boy, I had accompanied Gaspar on several of his visits there and knew this girl had disappeared several months ago. I had wondered about her absence, as I was aware of most comings and goings, but knew not whether she had been ransomed, traded or stolen - but here she was, and I knew I could not leave without her.

I grabbed Swift and led him back down the game trail we had followed to the camp. At the river, he started talking, but I hushed him and moved toward the water where I waded around several bends and overhanging cypress branches before I stopped and waited for him to catch up. I hoped he had not seen her.

"Well, what now?" he asked.

"We find their canoes and then go back to the beach and make a plan."

"Looked like those men were well armed," he said.

"I didn't see any guns, and I'm not planning on waiting for them to return," I said and moved along the river bank making better time now that we could walk along the shore. We carried our boots and moved barefoot in the sand so as not to leave a trail. Within minutes, we reached the boats and I went to check on Rhames.

He was leaning against a boat drinking water from a coconut shell when I approached.

"What'd you see," he asked.

"Men went off hunting. There are some canoes by the water. I think we ought to make our move now and get upriver before the men get back," I said as I went to him and removed the torn shirt binding his wound. It looked better; the puss had dried, and the dark edges looked red now. I went for a fresh coconut and to gauge the strength of the other men. It would be another day with little rest, but I knew as long as we had the treasure they would make it. Staying here was too dangerous with this large a tribe nearby, and this was the perfect chance to take the canoes - and Rory.

When I returned, he allowed me to recoat the wound with more coconut oil and rebind it. "We go now?"

"You should stay with the boats," I said.

"Bloody hell," he replied.

I knew it was a waste of breath to fight with him, but I needed to tell him about the other problem I faced and leaned toward him. "There's a girl from Captiva there and I mean to take her with us."

Chapter Two

We moved as a group toward the Indian camp. Rhames had the pistol and had agreed to guard our rear after several minutes of heated discussion. He was accustomed to leading these forays, but had finally agreed to watch our backs. I had to admit as I looked behind us to check on him that I was impressed a little by my doctoring skills. I had cleaned and wrapped the wound with fresh linen before we moved out, and I could see no sign of blood or discharge on his shirt.

The mention of the girl had not gone over well with him or the other men, but in the end they were pirates and used to taking what they wanted without permission. If I wanted to rescue the girl, it would be my task alone.

We retraced our steps, barefoot along the sand. I suspected some of the tribe's more experienced trackers could tell the difference between our footprints and theirs, but the more we could do to hide our presence the better. As we approached the overhanging cypress tree, I held up my hand to halt the group.

"Swift knows where the boats are. Follow him, take three and destroy the rest."

"And you?" Red asked.

"I'm going for the girl. Get the canoes and head back to our camp. Leave me one canoe and tow the others with the longboats. Until the river forces us to abandon them, we can make better speed with the oars than the push poles they use for the canoes. Go, I'll catch up."

I moved inland before they could argue. Rhames had led them through more dangerous raids than this and I had to believe they would succeed without me. Careful to hide my movements I followed the game trail we had used earlier and reached the camp unnoticed. The men were nowhere in sight, and there were fewer women and children in the clearing than earlier. I suspected they had gone to forage or work some crops that were further inland.

Mosquitos swarmed, and I coated my exposed skin with mud and dirt hoping to fend them off, but they continued unabated. I tried to ignore the bugs and focus on my mission. Rory was a prisoner, brought here against her will. Whether abducted or sold it didn't matter at this point. She was able-bodied and would surely be forced to pull her weight and work with the stronger women.

I moved back down the game trail and stopped short as it ended in a clearing. Through the rows of corn, I could see several figures working. From this distance, I couldn't tell if Rory was one but I needed to check. I moved fast now, staying in the rows, using the height and density of the plants to hide my approach. As I got closer, I heard talking and slowed to listen. I couldn't make out the language but used the noise to guide me to a section they had already harvested and peered around the corner.

There she was, pulling the ripe ears from the stalks and placing them in a basket at her feet. Two women were nearby, working and talking. Neither paid attention to the girl as they felt no threat. Their biggest concern was that she worked. On my knees now, I crept toward her stopping every few feet to listen. A few minutes later I found myself in the adjacent row.

"Rory - Don't look," I whispered.

I could see her tense and stoop, her head moving back and forth. I thought she was about to call the other women when she bent over. "Who are you that knows my name?"

"It's Nick. From Gaspar's crew," I said.

"The Devil!" she hissed.

I had not thought of the possibility that she hated us as much as her current captors. "No, I'm the cabin boy. They took me several years ago too," I pleaded with her.

"So you say. But at least these savages haven't raped me."

This was going badly, and I needed to convince her before the other women suspected anything. "I'm not like that. I want to help you. At least get you back to civilization where you can make your own choices."

She continued her work for a long minute. "And how do you suppose to rescue me?"

"You're going to have to trust me. There's not enough time now to tell you all that has happened." I stopped not knowing how much to tell her now. "I want to help you."

"Right. Here's the cabin boy wanting to help me. That's nice - probably get us both killed in the process."

"I've got men and boats," I said and took a chance. She had to come willingly, or we would lose all notion of stealth. "Please. We have to go now." I made like I was moving away to force her decision.

She spoke several words to the other women, and I thought for a second she had turned me in, but as I was about to run, she appeared at my side.

"Well? You have a plan?"

"But, the women. What did you tell them?" I asked.

"Told them I needed to pass some water."

My heart jumped in my chest and I looked at her. Afraid I would lose my voice if I spoke, I started moving back toward the game trail.

She followed until we reached the trail, then stood with her hands on her hips. "Where are we going?"

"We have a camp upriver," I said and turned back to the trail.

"And when they find you?"

I looked back and faced her, shrugged and turned away.

"It's not too late for me to go back you know. At least I know what I'm dealing with here. You could have one of those bastards at your camp just waiting to rape me again."

I hadn't considered this twist either. Cleary she was thinking better than I, and I admitted to myself that all I wanted was for her to be with me. "What's it going to take to persuade you that I want to help?" I tried to put the onus on her.

She was silent for a minute, and I grew anxious.

"Swear to me that you mean no harm."

"I do," I said.

She moved toward me and my heart jumped. "Let's go. Better the devil I know than these heathen."

We moved to the beach and reached the cypress tree where we waded into the water, and I saw her look back.

She turned back to me, "Well Nick. If this is it then here we go."

I couldn't contain my smile and was sure she saw me blush as I trudged through the water to get around the tree and headed toward our camp. We traveled in silence, each taking cautious looks over our shoulders. Around a corner, I breathed a sigh of relief when I saw the nose of a canoe sticking out of the brush. I hurried to it and pulled the line holding it from a branch.

"Hurry," I said looking back to the camp. There had been no sign so far that they had realized she was gone, but by now enough time had passed they would be looking.

"What about the camp and your men?"

"They took the other boats and went upriver. We'll find their camp by dark."

"Upriver is it? That's odd."

"It's a bit of a story and I'll be happy to tell you once we're on the water. But we need to move. They're sure to have noticed you gone by now." I climbed into the stern of the boat and grabbed the long pole from the bank.

She waded toward me and again I was stung by her beauty. Her skirts parted and revealed her legs as she climbed over the side. Turning away, I grabbed the pole with both hands and pushed against the mucky bottom. The shaft stuck and I pulled to no avail.

"Good Lord," She said as she hopped over the side, took the pole, and rocked it back and forth until it came free. "Move forward. I guess I'll be rescuing you."

I moved to the bow and again caught a glimpse of her bare leg as she climbed in. With one hand down the shaft and the other near the top she set the pole at a low angle and pushed. The canoe started to move forward, picking up speed with each long push. Soon we were well down the river.

"You gonna let the girl do all the work?" she asked as she stopped pushing, handed me the pole and moved to the front of the canoe.

I took her vacated position and did my best to mimic her motions as I pushed us forward. It was awkward at first, but after a dozen or so attempts I caught on. Now to find the camp and hope that none of my men were the ones that had raped her.

Chapter Three

She sat quietly in the bow of the boat as I poled us upriver. The current was mild and the work easy once I got the movement figured out. I had a hard time taking my eyes off her, although I did risk a glance back every few minutes. Deer scattered from the banks as we approached and alligators in larger numbers than I had ever seen sunned themselves on the sandy shore.

I knew Rhames would want to put as much distance between our camp and the Indian village as possible before stopping, but I was getting anxious as we only had an hour until dark, and there was still no sign of them. My stomach rumbled, and my throat burned. Food would have to wait, but at least the water flowed clear here so we could drink our fill from cupped hands when we stopped for a break.

"Where's your band of men, Captain Nick?" She turned and looked at me. "Surely you have one and it not just the two of us."

I saw her eyeing my cutlass and dagger, the only weapons we had.

"And that's what we've got to fight off the savages? You know they'll come after us. Where they got it I have no idea, but I saw the gold they exchanged for me."

My curiosity piqued. I had wondered about her circumstance, and this was the first clue she had given. "They didn't hurt you or - you know," my voice faltered.

"Oh. In that regard, they were nicer than your band of buffoons. Blonde hair and blue eyes - I'm worth a fortune in trade or favor to them as I am." She turned back to watch the river ahead.

I was about to ask more, but the river turned on itself, and I saw a longboat pulled ashore on the far bank. "There they are," I said with more confidence than I felt. There was no telling what might happen when she saw them, or they saw her. I had a powder keg on my hands and no idea how long of a fuse it had.

With a long, hard push, I grounded the boat and jumped to the dirt beach. I breathed a sigh of relief as I saw the other boat and canoes further around the bend. I heard voices from behind the brush where the plume of smoke from a small fire was barely visible.

I pushed my way through two palmetto palms, cursing as I cut my forearm on a stray branch and entered the clearing. "What! No watch and a fire?" I looked around at Red, Swift, Johnnie, and Syd. "Where's Rhames," I asked as I looked back at the men to see if they had the pistol aimed at me.

"Over by the boats. Probably sleeping," Red said. "Tough bastard - that one."

"Finish cooking and get that fire out before dark. We need to move and put more water between us and them before we stop for the night." I said.

"Aye, but they've no boats. We trashed and holed the canoes left behind. They won't be coming by water," he said.

"Truth be told we don't know how or with what force they will come after us with, but they will." I didn't need to say anything else as Rory entered the clearing and caught the eyes of the men.

I watched their reaction, trying to gauge if any would be trouble when I saw Johnnie flinch. Was it in recognition, or did he feel the same things that I did when I looked at her? She walked toward the fire and took a piece of meat off the branch that was holding it over the fire. We had smoked all the turtle so there would be no need to cook that. I looked around the clearing and saw the carcass of a four-foot gator, then turned to the sky thankful that no buzzards had sensed it as they would alert the Indians to our location.

The meat appeared cooked, and I doused the fire using the hard base of a dead palm frond as a shovel. "I need to check on Rhames," I said to the group, then looked at Rory, who I hoped would follow and walked out of the clearing toward the boats.

He sat in the stern of one of the longboats, propped against the seat. His eyes were wide open; a vacant look on his face and I had a moment of panic as I thought he was dead. Finally he snapped out of his trance, looked at the girl, but spoke to me, "See you've found a bit of trouble there, boy."

"It had to be done. I couldn't leave her with those heathens." I replied unsure how a real pirate would have acted.

"Aye, but now we've got more trouble than Lafitte and the Navy," he sat up.

"We should have lost them by now. No one goes this far upriver."

He turned his gaze to me, "No one but a bunch of pirates with treasure. They'll follow us through the gates of Hell for what we've got in these chests."

I turned to the chests. "Right. So we should move out," was all I could think to say. It seemed that leading was much easier when we were moving than when we were camped.

"Think we might at least want to know who's after us? If they're fighters and how they're armed," he asked.

"How would we know?" I asked and shrunk as I watched him turn toward Rory.

"Got a name, girl?" he asked.

"Rory," she responded. "And they are properly equipped to fight you. They hunt with the bow, but they have firearms."

I watched her recount their manpower and armaments feeling stupid as I had spent most of the day fixated on her beauty and ignoring her brain. As she told Rhames about their ways, I swore I would not make the same mistake again.

"Hear that, boy? We've got plenty of trouble on our hands. I figure rowing against the river and pulling the canoes that we made ten miles today. They know the land and even without boats they can be on us in minutes."

I did the math in my head and realized he was right. A war band knowing their footing could easily make three, maybe four miles an hour. The head start I thought we had was gone.

"Can you travel," I asked him.

"Aye. Get the men."

I watched his face and saw a twinge as he repositioned himself, but there was nothing to be done. "Stay with him," I told Rory and went back to the clearing to get the men.

They must have sensed my urgency because they were already packed up and ready to leave. In minutes, we loaded the boats and were ready to push off. I felt the need to stay close to Rhames and Rory, and we took a longboat hoping she could row as well as she handled the canoe.

"I can row," she said and sat by the port oar.

The other men sorted themselves out; two in the longboat pulling the canoes, and the other two pushed us off the bank before taking the canoe that Rory and I had brought. I was impressed again watching Rory row. I kept watch behind us and cursed as I noticed the first buzzard circle the camp.

"What's that you're thinking?" She asked.

Rhames cut me off, "The bird. It'll surely attract the Indians."

"Any luck it'll be dark before they see it," I said as I watched the sun break the horizon behind us. As it sank, I noticed the grunts of the gators from the banks as they slid into the water for their evening hunt. I knew we were safe behind several inches of oak, and I tried to ignore them as we moved upriver.

I tried to quiz Rory about the geography here as we rowed, but we were well past the extent of her travels. The hours slipped numbly by as we ate up miles of water and I was in the kind of trance a man can fall into when working monotonous labor. I lost my oar and my body shot forward.

Chapter Four

I regained my balance and looked around the dark water, not sure if I had been asleep. There was a small moon hanging in the east, but it provided little light. My first thought had been that we were under attack, but I soon saw that we had just hit a cypress stump. Its gnarly head stuck from the water, and I realized how the features of the river had changed. It was narrow and shallow here, not like the wide and deep river we had entered. Moss hung from the trees just above our heads dropping the occasional insect as we brushed it.

The other long boat in front of us was also having trouble moving through the cluttered river, but the canoe manned by the other men was having no trouble navigating. The pole was able to pick its way around the obstructions, where the oars extending from the long boats were unable to gain purchase on the water.

"Pull to the side," I called to the boats surprised by how easily my voice carried in the night. It was past time to abandon the worthless oars, and I slid over the side. As we neared the bank, the bottom sucked at my feet, but as I pulled the boat to the beach the footing became more secure. Behind me, Red was also in the water pulling the other longboat ashore. The brush came within a few feet of us, and we had to fight to beach the boats. "We'll never get through with these. It's time to abandon them," I said and looked at the river.

"The boats?" Red asked.

"We've got the canoes. That's what they're made for." I peered inland knowing we would have to drag the longboats out of sight to ditch them. Several sets of eyes glowed from the darkness and I wondered what lived in these woods. We had seen deer and gators along the bank and heard larger animals. There were rumors of big cats called panthers, as well as bears. "Pull everything out of the longboats and hide those canoes out of sight,"

The darkness was broken as the sun climbed above the horizon. I grabbed my cutlass from the boat and checked that the dagger was still secure in my belt. As I entered the woods, I extended the blade of the sword in front of me to move the hanging moss aside and to cut away the tangles of berry bushes.

The sun started to light the area in front of me as I moved through the dense brush lining the river. Ten feet in, the bank rose a few feet to its high water mark and the brush thinned as I climbed from the river bed. Cypress trees were scattered about, but the thorny berry bushes were gone, and the palmettos were in clumps making the walking easier. Slashing several tree trunks as I went to mark the path for my return, I searched for any sign that men traveled along these shores. The flora thinned further as I walked making it easier to see the landscape. The sky was light, and I scanned the ground for any tracks - left by either man or animal and found none. A small depression covered in palmettos lay ahead. It was the only break in the land, and I hoped it was deep enough to hide the boats. I would have preferred to burn them and bury the metal fittings, but the smoke would signal our presence.

I reached the depression and hacked away the closest leaves. It was several feet deep, the bottom lined with standing water and covered with berry bushes. I snatched at the fruit and paused to enjoy the berries and catch my breath. The area was large and deep enough to hold the boats and I expected the berry bushes would quickly envelope them making them all but invisible. I grabbed another handful and started back to camp.

The chests were unloaded and stacked on the shore along with our meager supplies when I returned. Rory was by Rhames, who lay next to one of the boats. She was tending his wound. The other men were all side by side, some asleep.

"Get up. We've got to get rid of the long boats." The sooner we got off the river the better. Although we were far from safe, I felt the miles we had paddled overnight may have given us enough time to hide the boats and erase our presence on the river. We all needed rest, and I planned on moving inland to camp.

"Right then," I said when I had their attention. "Let's move the chests into the brush and drag the canoes clear of the shore. There's a spot a few hundred yards inland that we can hide the longboats. Then we can rest." The men muttered in discontent, but I knew they understood the urgency. Minutes later the beach was cleared and I watched as Rory took two palmetto leaves and raked the thin slice of dirt. The Indians had reputations as trackers, but if they somehow had followed by water I was sure they would see no sign of us here. I planned on camping further inland than any likely land route would take them as an extra precaution. "Rory, stay with Rhames and watch the chests. You men, we need to drag the longboats over there." I went to the first boat and started to pull, but it refused to move. The weight of the heavy oak boats was going to make it impossible to move them.

"They ain't moving," Red reinforced what I had already determined. "And what about the chests he asked."

Our priority was to get the longboats away from the river and out of sight. I would have to figure out what to do about the treasure after that. “One thing at a time.” I looked around for a solution to my immediate problem of how to move the boats. Several bare limbs on the ground tugged a memory loose from my mind. “Grab those limbs and cut a few more.” I didn’t wait but went for the limbs and started cleaning the small branches from them. The first was now smooth, about the height of a man and as thick as his wrist. “Come on. We need two more this size.”

I took the logs to the first boat and placed one several feet in front of it. “Lift the boat and slide these under. One at the bow and the other at the stern,” I said.

The boat sat on the logs and we as one we pushed it onto the log in front. It took several tries to get into a rhythm with two men on either side of the boat pushing it and me moving the logs to keep it rolling. We covered the distance and pushed the boat into the depression. The men ate berries and rested while I surveyed our work. It was barely visible from a few feet away. Once the bushes grew, it would be totally concealed. The other boat soon joined it in the shallow grave, and we went back to where Rhames and Rory sat and made camp.

Chapter Five

I decided to take first watch on the river and set a schedule until morning. We badly needed rest, and though it was possible the Indians were still in pursuit, without their canoes and with no sign of trails nearby, I thought we might finally be safe. The men and Rory were fed and scattered around the camp resting. As I left, I glanced back at Rory and Rhames together by one of the canoes. She seemed to gravitate toward him and was again checking his wound. She caught my eye and cast a worried look. I ordered that no fires be lit and walked toward the river. I would check on Rhames after my watch.

I tried to think of our next move, but thoughts of the girl kept creeping into my mind. Unable to push them aside, I sat on the small dirt beach, and thankful for the shade, leaned against the trunk of a cypress tree. It was midday and the adrenaline from the rescue had long worn off. Even in the shade it was hot, and I was lulled to sleep, the only activity, the birds chirping and the river moving slowly by.

The sound of a man singing caused me to open my eyes. Not sure if it was a dream or not, I stood and moved toward the water where the sound seemed to come from. It was getting louder and closer. The loaded pistol was in my hand as I used the brush as cover and crept to the water. The song continued, and I saw the bow of a canoe move around the bend.

Had the boat been coming from the coast as we had, I might have let it go, but it was floating downriver, and we desperately needed to know what lay ahead. The rest of the boat came into view, and I saw a single man standing in the bow gracefully poling the canoe. He appeared an odd character, dressed in what would once have been fancy clothes but were now tattered and faded. On his head, an old top hat was cocked to one side which almost fell off his head when I stepped out of the bushes and pointed the pistol at him.

"Buenos Dias, mi amigo," he called out and poled the canoe to the shore.

I ignored his friendly manner and kept the gun pointed at him. "English?"

"And some of the heathens tongue as well," he responded with an accent.

"Who are you and what's your business on the river?" I asked in my most threatening voice. As I waited for his answer, I moved closer to inspect his canoe. It was full of trade goods: trinkets and clothes. A long gun was the only visible weapon. I took two quick steps and grabbed it. "That your only weapon?"

"I've a dagger as well," he answered.

"Let's have it then. Pull the boat to the shore and move over to that rock," I pointed with the pistol to where I wanted him. I froze for a second when he reached under a pile of clothes. At first I thought I might have underestimated him, and there would be something more dangerous there, but he was good to his word and tossed the small knife onto the sand by my feet. In no rush, he pulled the boat onto the beach and went to the rock.

I stood several feet from him facing the water in case more boats were following. "Well friend, what brings you here?" I tried to relax my demeanor.

"I'm just a trader. Work the river from the big lake to the ocean trading what I can with who I can."

"And what of the rumor about a river of grass that runs into the Keys."

"You must be in some desperate straits if you're looking at that route."

I was just about to ask for more details when I saw his gaze move to the bushes and the look on his face changed to panic. Before I could turn to see what had alarmed him, I heard someone move behind me and grab the pistol from my side. The gun fired before I could react, and the man fell over, a red spot forming on his chest.

"Bastard!"

She pulled the trigger again, but nothing happened, then threw the pistol down and went for the dagger. I grabbed her, and we wrestled, landing with a thump on the ground. She fought back, but my weight subdued her. "We need him." I tried to reason with her.

"Bastard!" She screamed again and fought with renewed vigor.

I kept my grip on her and stole a glance at the man. "Well, the bastard's dead," I said as I rolled off her.

She sat up and looked at him with a wild look on her face. "He's the one that sold me," she said as tears streamed down her face.

Not sure whether she would reject me if I went to comfort her after our struggle, I remained where I was and waited for her to compose herself. "He said he was a trader," I said and realized my mistake as soon as the words left my mouth.

She glared at me, and I looked away. "He made a deal with one of your mates. They came for me one night, and I saw the gold change hands as he bound me and then took me to the Indian camp."

I was so focused on her and her story that I failed to notice the other men standing behind me. They must have heard the shot and came to investigate.

"Got a mess here," Rhames said from behind them. "You two, get the body out of here. The others can drag the canoe back toward camp and clean up the beach."

I realized he was doing my job. "Swift, take the watch," I said as I stood up and brushed the dirt from my clothes. Rory was still sitting, and I reached for her. "Come on. What's done is done. Let's go back to camp and sort this out." She took my offered hand and rose.

"Did he work alone?" I asked her as we stood in a circle. I was worried that if he had accomplices they might be on the river as well.

"Yes," she muttered finally meeting my eye.

The group relaxed with her statement. We had a watch on the river in case there were more, but it appeared, unless someone distant heard the gunshot that we would remain unnoticed.

I went to the canoe and started piling the clothes and trinkets on the ground. Many Indians favored our style of clothes and he probably did good business trading with them. As I pulled out the last coat, I saw the dull glint of metal hidden below it. I withdrew two pair of handcuffs, spotted with blood and held them for the group to see. I looked over at Rory, but she was looking down. The men seemed to murmur approval at what she had done.

The hull was nearly empty when I discovered an oilskin folder. I opened the flap and removed several hand drawn maps. One I recognized immediately as the area around Gasparilla Island and the other looked unfamiliar. I only took a minute to realize it was a map of the area we sought to travel; the big lake labeled Mayaca. It showed the shores and a small river exiting from the south. I knew from the sun that we were traveling east and knew the southern outlet was the river of grass.

Chapter Six

It's a different feeling having arrows fly over your head when you are used to steel weapons and inaccurate firearms. The projectiles whistled as they passed overhead and thumped when they struck in the dirt or a tree. We huddled in a small cove, our backs to the beach, using the overturned canoes as a barricade. Our group had been quiet and on alert since the incident with the trader yesterday. Aside from the circumstances surrounding his demise and the loss of the information unspoken from his lips, it was almost a blessing. A crew suspicious and looking for any unusual activity was easier to manage than a bored band of pirates.

We had combined all the treasure into four heavy chests which allowed us to transport them one to a canoe. It was an awkward arrangement but the only one we had. With the trader's vessel, we now had four canoes, six men, and Rory. At dawn yesterday we had pushed off the shores of the river after carrying the two empty chests to the depression where the boats were stashed. We then set the trader in a shallow grave to avoid the tell-tale buzzards that would seek out his rotting flesh.

I had studied the map and memorized any distinguishing feature before we had left. The problem was that Rory had killed the trader before he could disclose our location on the river. Another few minutes with the man might have saved us from our present situation as I feared we had come up on the lake and the large village marked there sooner than we expected. Had I known this we would have set up a camp further downriver and sent scouts to the river mouth.

Although we had been vigilant, the smoke from the fires in the village was invisible, and the Indians were capable of more stealth than we gave them credit. We had rounded a bend and seen a group of men move from the bushes with bows drawn. Before we could react, the air was full of arrows, and we took cover in the hollowed-out cypress of our boats holding our coats over our heads to stave off the arrows. Fortunately, although their aim was good, the distance prevented the arrows from striking with much velocity.

As the arrows flew, I started to take in our surroundings in the waning sunlight. The minutes passed, and the shadows grew longer and the smoke visible to our right and upriver marked the location of the village. I pulled the map from its oilcloth holder and tried to ascertain our position relative to the Indian camp. The village was shown on the southern bank of the river just before it emptied into the lake. We were taking fire from a small band of fighters on the opposite side of the river from the village. I turned away from the attackers and suspected their ploy.

"They aim to pin us down here and my guess is they will attack from behind us as soon as the sun sets." I looked inland trying to judge where they would come from and how to defend ourselves. "Least they don't have firearms," I said.

Rhames shot me a look, "Don't be so sure. They may be holding them in reserve. That's what I would do. They know from this distance they would be ineffective. Bastards just want to pin us down."

I saw no way out. "We have to take a chance and get back on the river before they attack," I called out.

"Aye, no choice there," Rhames backed me up.

As yet we had offered no defense, but we would need to use the pistol and rifle to cover our exit. I planned it in my head and got an idea from the thick moss hanging from the cypress trees. "Help me with this," I asked Rory, who was almost entirely inside one of the hulls, the fear of being recaptured by the Indians clear in her eyes.

She was frozen in place so I tapped Red on the shoulder, and he followed me as I crawled to the nearest tree. The moss hung to within a few feet of the dirt, and I was able to reach up and pull a large clump of it without revealing myself. Branches swayed as I did, but the aim of the archers remained on the cluster of boats. I kneeled in the dirt and started wrapping myself in the dense and fibrous moss, starting at my head and winding it around my neck and then my body. Red reached out to touch me, and as I hoped, the material appeared to be thick enough to repel an arrow, at least from the distance they were shooting.

We both gathered armloads of moss and returned to the group who surrounded us with scared and questioning faces. "As soon as the sun dips behind those trees we need to move out. They'll come from the land behind us, as soon as it gets dark. Use the moss like this." I showed my technique, "With any luck we'll blend into the river."

Heads nodded, and two other men helped collect enough moss to cover both ourselves and the boats. If we were quiet in the dim light I hoped we would be invisible to the attackers. The deep shadows cast from the moss-covered trees gave the illusion of twilight and the quantity of arrows dwindled to several a minute as we wrapped ourselves from the waist up. I knew the land-based attack would likely come soon, and we braved the intermittent arrows to right the boats, drape moss over their sides and load the chests and supplies.

Minutes later we were ready.

I had been so involved in preparing the boats that I failed to notice the arrows had stopped, a sure sign the attack was imminent. "Into the boats," I called out and waded into the water pushing the first boat in front of me. I didn't wait for the others. They knew the urgency of the situation, and I soon heard the men behind me.

Just as my pole hit the sandy bottom and the boat moved into the channel I heard activity on the shore and a woman scream. I looked back and in the fading light could see Rory standing ankle deep in the water surrounded by Indians. I cursed myself for not keeping an eye on her, but there was nothing we could do as arrows rained down on us from the shore as they led her inland.

Chapter Seven

We absorbed a flurry of arrows as we poled the boats past the far bank, but the moss held and although we could feel the arrows strike, they did not reach our skin. Soon, the only notion of our passing was the barely audible sound of the poles as they occasionally scraped against the wooden hulls. Our camouflage was so convincing that as twilight turned to night I had to struggle to see the canoe in front of ours. I watched behind us and scanned both banks of the river for any activity, but there was no movement or sound. Although capable of stealth, the Indians had no need for it now - they had the woman. The moon was a quarter up the sky when we finally decided to stop and pulled our cutlasses and guns out. We were all aware of each other and our surroundings as the bottoms of the burnished cypress boats scraped against the gravelly bottom.

We hopped out and gathered in a small group glad to remove the moss we had used to protect and conceal us. If there were Indians here I figured there was no harm in it - we would be dead already. I took my covering and placed it back in the boat while watching several others do the same.

"Why are we stopping so close to the bastards?" Red asked.

"Ya. There's no reason. What if they come after the treasure?" another commented.

"You can do what you want. I'm not leaving here without Rory," I had figured this was going to happen and had no other answer.

"Boy's got a case of it, I guess. What about you Rhames. You're awfully quiet over there," Red said.

Rhames was still covered in moss and only the occasional flash of moonlight reflecting off the metal rifle barrel revealed his position. I made a note to tarnish the steel of our weapons. We watched him, wondering if we were indeed safe or should replace the moss we had taken off when he came toward us.

"Someone's been here," he said as he took the moss from his head and sat on the bow of one of the canoes.

He looked sick, and I remembered the pained look on his face before I took the watch and discovered the trader. We had been moving non-stop since then, and I had failed to check on him.

"Looks like about ten men camped here," Red said. "There's a fire pit, cold now, but the embers are still there, so they were here after the rain."

I thought back to the rain and realized it was only a handful of days ago. "Why would a group camp here when the main village is only an hour or so away?"

"Now you're thinking," Rhames said but stopped trying to mask the pain on his face.

I started running scenarios in my mind. Had the party been made up of Indians from the village close by, they either would not have camped here or would have built the fire on the open beach. There were rumors that the Army was rounding up the Indians in the North to secure them on reservations out West and those who chose to fight were fleeing South and taking refuge in this area. But Army scouts would have left no trace, and a larger company would have been well armed and had no need to conceal themselves.

Suddenly, we looked up and found several rifles cocked and we were surrounded by a dozen men. Before we could react, a dark-skinned man dressed in once fancy pants, a dress shirt, and bowler hat moved forward to take our guns. As I looked at the group, they were all dressed in similar fashion; the only native clothing was the moccasins on their feet. European blood was clearly evident in their features - a mixture of Creek Indian and whoever was hunting, trapping or trading on their lands at the time.

One man moved forward. "Who leads you?" he asked in English, clearly his native tongue.

I moved forward.

He laughed, "A boy?"

I looked at him and realized we were of the same age. "And you look no older than me."

He ignored the comment and shocked me when he extended his hand in the fashion recently made popular by Thomas Jefferson. "I am Osceola."

I gave him my name, moved toward him, took his rough hand in mine and squeezed. "Are you the Seminoles?" I asked.

"We are. I lead my tribe. And you look to be outlaws or pirates," he said.

I saw his eyes move toward the boats lit in the moonlight and followed his gaze, thankful that we had left the moss covering the chests. He looked back at me.

"And what is a bunch of white pirates doing so far inland?"

I told him briefly of our escape from the Navy and run-in with the tribe just downstream. For the time being I kept the rescue and abduction of Rory to myself not knowing how they would react.

"You run from Andrew Jackson as well?"

So we were allied in that regard. I had heard the name, but didn't know how it applied to us. "Yes. The Navy is after us."

The Indians still held their rifles, but they lowered their weapons. Several of the men were grouped in the area that Rhames had found the fire, and I saw the spark of a flint. "No fires," I said. "We just had a run-in with the Indians downstream."

"Interesting. From what I have heard they wouldn't want trouble from a small band of white men. They would let the land deal with you." He looked at me.

"Truth be told, we stole these canoes from a band further downstream and rescued a woman they had hostage." There was no use lying to him. I suspected that we would need their help if we were to rescue Rory.

He left me standing there and went to his men by the fire. Our group came together whispering questions to each other, as we watched the Indians gather and do the same. They knew nothing of the treasure, or we would probably be dead, broke, or both already. What we shared and the reason we might still be standing was we had a common enemy in the United States Government. Somehow I needed to work this to our advantage. Before I had an answer, they broke their huddle and Osceola came toward me.

"We will help you get the woman back. It seems we have more in common than avoiding Andrew Jackson."

Before I could ask, he explained.

"This land here, where the river meets the big lake is the only habitable spot that we can both protect and thrive in. The tribe that lives here has rejected our offers of peace and we were on our way back to wait for our warband. We have no choice but to deal with them if we want to survive. They claim to be original Calusa with pure bloodlines and look at us as outcasts with mixed blood. I have tried to explain that we are the same and share the same enemies, but they rejected us. Now we must do what we need to survive."

I understood his plight, being from mixed blood myself. Although my family claimed to be Dutch, we had a line of Semitic blood that forced us to immigrate rather than being persecuted. I suspected Osceola shared the same fate with his mixed heritage. "But how can we help? We are just a handful of poorly armed pirates."

He slapped my back, "My new friend. We will see."

Chapter Eight

Osceola sent scouts on foot both up and downriver to see if the other tribe was stalking us, but both groups came back several hours later and reported no sign of the other tribe. Apparently the abduction of Rory had satisfied them, and they were content to let us go. Osceola had no answer for whether the tribe we stole the canoes and liberated Rory from and the tribe that held her now were related. I suspected they were as this was the first we had heard of Seminoles this far south. It also made sense that they controlled, travelled, and traded along the length of the entire river, meaning we would not only have to deal with them to free the girl, but also to gain access to the big lake.

We started several fires after his men returned to cook and keep warm. The temperature had plummeted, and I noticed a haze around the moon; a sure sign the weather was about to change. He told me of his struggle with the Army, and I recounted the tale of our escape from the Navy as well as our plans to head south through the river of grass to the Keys.

At this, he laughed, "You pirates, are going to stumble your way into the mouth of a waiting alligator. Not one of you is a tracker or guide."

I gave him an odd look, "All we have to do is head south, and we will end up at the tip of the peninsula." I pulled the map from my pocket and showed him our intended route.

He took the parchment and studied it. "You have no idea what lies between here and there," he pointed at the map. "The Indians here say there are miles and miles of pointed grass they call sawgrass and water. No landmarks. There is talk that no one has ever made that journey and lived to tell of it. I fear if you go that way alone there will be six fewer pirates in the world," he laughed again.

I found no humor in his remarks. "And what would you suggest?"

"Here again I can help you. But first we must deal with the threat at hand."

"I thought your scouts said they weren't looking for us," I said.

He looked at me as a father to a son, "They are not looking for us because they know we are here."

He leaned back as if this thought did not trouble him. "So what do you have in mind?"

"If I were their leader, I would send a message to the village on the big lake that you are heading that way. We're between them. The tribe at the lake will come downriver, and the other will come upriver to try and squash us." He slapped his hands together like he was swatting a bug and laughed.

"You don't seem worried."

"I have a hundred warriors at my back. You have given us the perfect opportunity to fight the battle that we must." He looked around the camp. "Blue," he called to a figure in the shadows.

A small black man came toward us with an even smaller woman beside him. How I had not noticed them before, I don't know and again felt that I had better improve my skill if we were to survive the Indians.

"This is Blue and Lucy. He's the best tracker I've seen. We are where we need to be and intend to go no further than the big lake. They are free spirits and won't want to stay. I told him of your journey, and he and Lucy are willing to lead you."

I was grateful, and it must have shown on my face.

"But it is at a cost. He will lead you and your men back to the Indian camp. You will create a distraction and burn it," he ordered. "If you can rescue your woman, so be it."

I put my head down to put on my best stone face to conceal my smile and negotiate, although I already had what I wanted and more. Osceola and his men were going to be the distraction I needed to get Rory back, and now we had a guide. What we didn't have were weapons.

"That is good, but we need guns. We have only one rifle and one pistol. To give you the time you ask for we will each need a rifle and powder."

He did not speak, and I thought I might have overplayed my hand, but a minute later his hand extended and we shook.

"We will set a watch and leave at midnight," he said and walked away. Blue and Lucy remained by me, and we passed an awkward moment in silence. I realize they were waiting for me to speak, "Osceola says you are the best tracker he knows," I said in as formal a voice as I could muster. "If you are willing, we would be grateful to have you both join us."

"That is good, Captain, but we are worried about trouble from your men," Lucy said.

I didn't understand at first; our crew had always had black men aboard, and they were treated as equals. "No worries there. You both will be equal members of our group."

They seemed to be reassured, and went back to where they had stood earlier, squatted down and picked up two satchels and a tube with a rope. They came back to us with their possessions. "We are with you," He said.

I needed to inform the crew of our additions and the plan that Osceola and I had agreed on. We moved away from the Indians and gathered together on a remote section of the beach to talk. The men were looking at Blue and Lucy when I broke the silence, "This is Blue and Lucy," I watched them as they turned to the newcomers checking each man's face before I spoke again. "Blue is a legendary tracker and guide. The rest of the Indians intend to stay here and fight the local tribe. He and Lucy want to move on."

I noticed Blue's smile when I added the legendary title. "We also have a deal with Osceola for weapons, but there are conditions."

"Always," someone murmured.

"I have to go back for Rory. Osceola has agreed to arm us if we go back to the village, hold them under fire for several hours and burn the village while he and his band go upriver and take the other tribe." I looked around for dissent.

Red stepped forward and said, "Figured you weren't leaving without her. If this one can guide us out of this mess and the Indian will give us weapons, then I'm in."

A chorus of "Ayes" came from the other men. But as I looked around at the group I noticed that Rhames was missing. "Where is Rhames?"

"Got himself a fever. Said to meet without him," Swift said.

I ran to where Rhames was huddled by a small fire and looked at him. He clearly wasn't right, his eyes glassy when he looked back at me. I realized it had been more than a day since I had checked his wound, and it must be infected. I went to him and eased him onto the ground before removing the bandage and saw the green and black filled edges of the wound staring back at me. I searched my brain for any remedy but came up blank. Just as I was about to abandon hope, Lucy pushed me aside.

She leaned down and checked the wound, then called for Blue to bring her a torch and her satchel. The wound illuminated, I could see the damage. Without a pause, she reached for the satchel and took out a small pot and a bag. Blue took the pot from her, filled it with water, and placed it on the hot coals slightly out of the fire. She emptied the contents of the bag onto her skirt and sifted through the small pouches for the one she was after and replaced the rest. Blue returned with the steaming water and she took a large pinch of a bark like substance and placed it in the water. A low hum came from her throat as she steeped the mixture and with a piece of her skirt she bathed the infected areas. When she was finished she handed the now cooled pot to Rhames and waited while he drank it.

"Can he move?" I asked her.

"The medicine will work, but it takes some time."

Time we did not have. Osceola had said a few hours and I expected from the activity in the camp that he was making ready for his assault and would expect us to provide the distraction we had agreed on.

"I think we have no choice. He will have to stay with the boats." I looked at the men. "Get ready," I said and went to find Osceola to secure the firearms.

Chapter Nine

Blue moved back and forth along the river bank, squatting often to check something none of us could see. We were in the boats, poling close to the bank and as quietly as possible, our newly acquired rifles close at hand. Lucy was in my canoe with Rhames and one of the chests her added weight had little effect on the boat already riding low in the water. The other canoes held one chest and two men. I thought the moss had done an adequate job of concealing the chests, but in case it hadn't, I glanced over my shoulder every few minutes to make sure we were not followed.

Suddenly Blue stopped and held a hand up, signaling us to stop. Those poling the canoes moved closer to the bank, the other men readied the rifles. He waved us over, and we beached the boats on a small beach. I looked around for any sign of life as we exited the canoes and pulled them into the brush to conceal them, but had to admit I had no idea what he sensed. The moss-covered chest caught my eye as I dropped some palmetto leaves on the canoe to conceal the bow still visible from the beach.

Once the boats were hidden, we huddled around Blue, who spoke quietly.

"Each one knows his task," he started. "Men are close and the village is less than a few minutes' walk."

We broke into two groups to execute our plan. Rhames stayed behind leaning against a cypress trunk, rifle in hand. He looked slightly better than before, but it was hard to tell with his stoic countenance. I had Lucy, Blue, and one of the men with me. It would be our job to create a diversion, rescue Rory and burn the village. We nodded to each other and split up. I looked back over my shoulder and watched Red, Swift, and Johnnie as they walked single file; rifles extended, along the shore. They would get as close as possible and hide by the village dock, waiting for the first sign of fire before taking two canoes and scuttling the rest.

Our exposed limbs became red and bloody from the palmetto leaves as Blue led us along a small game trail more suitable for rabbits than men. Soon we could hear activity and see the flames of a fire high above the trees. I had heard about Indian ritual and suspected this was a pre-war celebration. He led us close enough to see the clearing through the brush and we squatted down to wait for an opportunity to present itself. I watched the men ready themselves for battle and assumed that they had trackers and knew of Osceola's presence and aims.

Blue came beside me, whispered in my ear that he would return shortly and silently moved away. I studied the clearing looking for any sign of Rory while he scouted the area. From where we hid, I could see most of the open area and started to worry as there was no sign of her. My anxiety increased thinking they may have moved her, or worse. I could do nothing but worry as I waited. As I reached my deepest feeling of despair and hopelessness, Blue startled me as he returned.

"The girl is held in that hut," he said in a low voice.

I followed his extended finger and noticed two men guarding the entrance to one of the thatched huts. The buildings were all identical, spaced around the clearing, their structures constructed from tree limbs and the walls and roofs covered with woven palm leaves. Swept dirt paths connected the buildings with each other and the clearing with the fire in the center. I worked through several scenarios to achieve our goals. "We need to start a fire away from her hut and draw the guards away," I whispered back.

"Is true. I will do that while you take another man and rescue your woman. We will meet at the boats." He tapped Lucy on the shoulder, and they moved silently away. In this phase of the operation, he was clearly in charge.

I watched him go and moved to Syd. "He is going to create a diversion. They are holding Rory in that hut," I pointed to the guarded house. "Follow me," I ordered and started pushing aside the razor sharp palm fronds. As we made our way through the brush, I could only hope that Blue wouldn't start the fire before we reached the hut.

It took twice as long as I thought to arrive at behind the structure, and I was again astounded at Blue's instincts as I saw a hut across the way start to smolder. Although it had rained hard the other night, the days this time of year were mostly dry, and the thatch caught in a whoosh. All eyes turned to the fire, and then everyone in the village went to extinguish the flames before they spread to the adjacent huts. We were behind the building and had to act quickly. Not knowing if the guards remained in front or had gone to fight the fire, I ordered Syd to cover me with the rifle while I withdrew my cutlass and hacked at the back wall of the structure. The thatch resisted my efforts, and I was soon breathing hard, partly from the exertion, but also from the fear of failure.

My plan to extract her from the hut from behind faltered, and I knew we would have to make a frontal assault. With my cutlass extended, I slid around the side wall to see if the guards were present and steeled myself for a close-quarters fight, something I was not comfortable with. The entry was unguarded, and I chanced a glance at the fire that had now spread to two other huts. Every man, woman, and child appeared to be fighting it. I hurried to the entrance, pushed aside the curtain with the edge of my sword and entered the hut.

The interior was dark, but I sensed more than one body. I shut my eyes for a second to try and acclimate them to the dim light. When I opened them, I saw a large figure lunge toward me. The inside of the hut was too small to swing the sword, so I did the only thing I was able. With my body braced I extended the cutlass to the figure and waited for contact. He must not have seen the sword, and I felt the impact and took his entire weight as he impaled himself and fell on top of me. Blood spurted as I released the sword handle and slid out from underneath his bulk. I looked around wildly trying to see if there was another threat, but felt a hand on my shoulder and saw Rory in front of me. She wiped her tears from her face and adjusted her clothing.

I stood staring at her, frozen for a moment until she spoke.

"Hurry. If you're here to rescue me, we better get on with it."

I gathered my wits and pulled the cutlass from the prone man. We looked at each other, and I nodded as she exited the hut. The fire still occupied the Indians, but I feared they would soon have it under control. "Wait here," I said as I ran toward the fire in the center of the clearing. If I could set fire to her hut, they might not find the dead man right away and assume she was burned alive. It would at least buy us some time. I reached the fire and grabbed a small log that I carried back to the hut and held it to the walls. It caught and I tossed the torch inside, grabbed Rory's hand and took off through the brush. I could only hope that Red and Swift had done their part.

Chapter Ten

We stumbled through the brush in the dark, blindly following Blue to the small beach where we had left the canoes. Slashed and bloody from the palmettos we reached the boats but Red and Swift were not there.

"Where are they?" I asked Rhames who sat unmoved by the cypress stump where we had left him.

"Don't know," he grimaced.

Lucy went toward him and checked his wound while Syd and I pulled the canoes from the brush and onto the shore. I looked up and saw the small outline of Blue against the shoreline, grabbed two rifles and took off after him after giving a stern warning to Syd to guard the women and Rhames. Confident we were not followed from the village, I caught up to Blue. He was working slowly around a bend in the river as if he had heard something, but it was difficult to see anything ahead of us, our night vision dulled by the bright flames of the fire.

He halted, and I felt a hand on my arm. I stood next to him using all my powers of observation, but I could not see or hear what disturbed him. We stood in the calf-deep water waiting for some unknown danger and I tried to hand him a rifle, which he refused. With one long gun slung over my shoulder, I readied the other and prepared myself. I heard the boat before I saw it and looked at the tracker who nodded. Then the bow of the first boat emerged from around the corner, and I saw Red and Swift each standing in a canoe poling frantically toward us.

I was about to call out to them when Blue squeezed my arm and pulled me out of sight. The two canoes passed, and I saw the cause for his concern. I heard a shot and a boat appeared. Blue caught my attention as I was about to fire and pushed the barrel of the rifle down. He had a long tube in his hand that he brought to his mouth, inhaled his cheeks filling with more air than they looked like they could hold and released his breath. A second later I heard a grunt and the man with the gun fell into the water. The man poling looked around, but his eyes, also blinded by the light of the fires didn't see us and passed by.

Suddenly two more canoes appeared, and Blue fired two more projectiles, hitting both helmsmen. The three unguided canoes started drifting downriver, back toward the village. As soon as they were back around the bend and out of sight, Blue tapped me again, and we hurried back to the clearing. The Indians would certainly regroup and follow.

We reached the clearing where we each grabbed a canoe, pulled it into the water and waited for Red and Swift as they pushed their boats to the bank. There was no need to exchange words, we all knew we had to move. I glanced over at Lucy and Rory, who were bent over Rhames, distressed looks on their faces. As I approached, I saw the wound was still bound, but a slimy green fluid penetrated the cloth and oozed onto his stomach.

"We have to move him," I said as I motioned to the other men to help.

"He looks near death," Rory whispered to me.

"Dead is what he'll be if we don't get him out of here. We slowed them down, but they are coming."

Syd and Swift moved in, each lifted an arm and draped it over their shoulder. With a nod, they lifted him from the ground and helped him to the boat.

"Leave me Nick. I'm done," he called out.

I was about to answer when Lucy cut me off, "White man will live. Medicine needs more time."

Relieved, but unsure of her prognosis I ignored his request and helped the men settle him into one of the empty canoes Red and Swift had taken from the village. I was about to step into the stern when Blue stopped me.

"You will need your guns. I will take him," he said and jumped in the boat. With the long pole, he pushed off the bank and started to move up the river.

We quickly sorted ourselves out and were soon in his wake. With four canoes, we were two to a boat. I placed the women in one boat, knowing that Rory could keep pace with most men. Swift and Red followed in another and Syd and I took the rear. He poled as I faced the stern, gun ready as I covered our escape. The fire was dying out now; its flames no longer visible over the trees.

I had been with Osceola as he drew out his plan to ambush the larger tribe in the dirt. He had drawn the village and showed each man, the leader of their groups, where to find cover. These were his chosen men who would take a small group of men and surround the village in the early morning, before the sun rose and attack as dawn broke on the signal of a single gunshot. I checked the river behind us again, but we had been moving steadily for several hours and I had seen nothing. I turned and started to watch ahead as a narrow band of light broke the horizon.

Just as I saw the first ray of sun, I heard the first shot. We were closer than I thought or wanted, and I urged the group to push harder. We had to get past the village and reach the lake while the battle raged. It was our only escape. Even with Osceola as an ally, he would likely discover our treasure if he did not already know of it. I looked ahead at Blue and wondered if he had been sent with us to spy for the chief.

Despite my paranoia, I knew we had no choice but to push on. The more distance we could place between us and both tribes the better our chances. Osceola, for all his help, would certainly seize the treasure at the first opportunity. I noticed our speed pick up and realized the group must have reached the same conclusion.

Smoke rose ahead of us, and the cries of a battle could be heard clearly now. Gunshots fired, steel clashed, and men screamed in both anger and pain as the two tribes met. Surrounded by moss and mist, we slipped by as if in a different world. As the noise faded behind us, the river gradually became wider and deeper. We had reached the lake, but there was no celebration. With Blue in the lead, we turned south; careful to stay far enough offshore to be out of arrow or gun range. We lashed the now useless poles to the boats and used the stocks of our guns to paddle. Two hours later, the battle well behind I felt safe enough to call for a break and pointed to a beach ahead.

We landed and looked at each other, exhausted from the night's work, but with adrenaline still running through our veins.

"Take some food and water," I called to the group as I stepped over the side of the boat and went to the women who were huddled over Rhame's body prone in the shell of a canoe.

TIDES OF FORTUNE

episode three

RIVER of GRASS

STEVEN BECKER

Chapter One

I tried to sleep, but finally gave up and took the watch around midnight. We had traveled what I expected was twenty miles, moving south and following the coast of the lake. It appeared our escape went unnoticed as we had slipped away during the battle. I hoped Osceola had won; he could be a valuable ally in the coming years. We had created a bond over the last few days, formed from our common age and flight from Andrew Jackson and the United States Navy. I didn't feel like a fugitive or that America was my enemy, but here we were.

The canoes were on the beach, the chests unloaded beside them. There was enough treasure for us to live like kings for years if we could only get someplace to spend it. I removed the trader's map from its oilskin case and placed it in front of me. As I studied it, I realized that if we kept our current pace, we would reach the southern end of the lake in two days, and then would enter the unknown.

I got up and walked to the water where I stared at the reflection of the moon on the lake and started thinking about our future. A voice startled me from my thoughts.

"What're you thinking?" Rory asked as she walked up and stood next to me.

She was tall for a woman but fell several inches short of my height. Her smell pleased me and I turned to her and noticed that she had bathed. Her hair was blonde and her skin glistened in the moonlight. She caught me off guard when she turned to me and smiled.

"Just planning our next move," I said and picked up a stone from the beach, wound up and released it. The small rock skipped once and disappeared into the dark water.

"I never thanked you for saving me," she said and skimmed her stone. It skipped three times before dropping.

The feeling of insecurity when she was close enveloped me again. There was something about her that started my heart and put a lump in my throat. "Anyone would have done the same," I said humbly.

"Well, thank you just the same."

We continued our unspoken contest in silence, the rocks making the only sound as they hit the water every few seconds.

"We should be out of the lake in a few days and into the river of grass," I threw again. "How is Rhames?" The first mate had been wounded right after our initial escape from the Navy. I had done my best to care for him, but he had relapsed yesterday. Now under the care of the pygmy woman, Lucy, I had kept my distance and let her doctor him.

"He was up and ate dinner. That's a good sign. The woman knows her medicine."

I thought back to our chance encounter with Osceola and his offer for weapons and the two pygmies in exchange for the diversion we had created allowing him to attack the Indian village. "And Blue as well," I said knowing that we would likely be dead without his tracking skills.

We were nine now; six of the original pirates plus Rory, Lucy, and

Blue. A smaller group would be easier to manage, but the additions of the escaped slaves and Rory each brought their own benefits. With four canoes, we had ample transportation, but I worried about the loaded chests making the boats top heavy. The canoes were the ideal vessel for the river and from what I suspected, for the river of grass as well. But the lake was bigger than any of us had imagined; the other side invisible. Even the light wind had driven small waves across the water, and I knew a larger blow would create waves large enough to capsize the unstable boats.

As the sky lightened across the water, a thin mist was visible on the lake. I suspected that as soon as the sun hit the water that fog would roll in. We spread palmetto leaves on the sand and sat, watching the sun rise.

"We better get on with it," I said and rose after a few minutes of silence. She followed me back to the camp. Blue was awake, whittling a branch into the shape of an paddle. I pursed my lips, realizing that I should have thought of that and had the men fashion paddles last night. Right after we had entered the lake, the poles we had used to push the boats through the river were lashed to the canoes and we had been using our gun stocks to move us through the water.

Rory went to Lucy, who was huddled over Rhames, a pot of steaming liquid by her side. I walked over to Blue and watched for a minute as he worked the wood, picked up another branch from the pile, withdrew my dagger, and started copying his movements. Soon the other men rose and started to stir the embers of the fire. Red and Swift joined us and as the smell of food drifted over to us, we had fashioned four crude paddles.

The group worked efficiently and by the time the fog lifted and the sun warmed the clearing we were fed. The boats were loaded and with each of us holding a crude paddle, we pushed off and climbed in. Rhames walked under his own power and pushed the last canoe into the water where he got in with a grunt. Shooting us a look to ward off sympathy, he grasped an oar and started paddling.

***

The landscape had changed in the last day as we continued south along the west bank of the river. It was our third day on the lake and we were moving swiftly. There had been no sign of pursuit, or any man for that matter and the group fell into an easy rhythm. The trees had thinned, the cypress and scrub oaks were still prevalent, but between the gaps in the woods we could see open space. That night we made camp knowing the next morning we would leave the lake and enter the river of grass.

As the men set up camp, I took stock of our supplies. The only thing left from the turtle we had caught was the shell, although there were what looked to be two days' worth of gator meat. I sat down and Rory came over as I studied the map.

"Looks like about the same distance to travel as the lake," she said as she leaned over my shoulder.

I had become more comfortable around her in the last few days, but her closeness brought the lump back to my throat. "It does. I expect there is some current that would favor us." The broad shaded area on the map between the big lake and the end of the peninsula showed no detail, just a vast blank area. I had no idea what to expect; whether there were areas of land or just an expanse of sawgrass standing above the water, hints of which we had seen through the gaps in the woods.

"I'm thinking we should stay here for a few days. We need to build up our food stores and I have no guess as to what we might find there," I pointed to the blank space on the map. "We can rest and reprovision here."

"Rhames could benefit as well. He is a stubborn one, but he's still weak. Lucy says the evil is out of him now."

I was thankful for the information. The last few days I had stayed away except for an occasional update and let the diminutive woman work on him.

"So, what lies ahead?" she asked.

"Miles of that," I pointed in the dark to our destination.

"That's not what I meant. What happens when we reach the Keys?"

I had spent hours during the monotonous time on the water thinking about the future while we moved along the lake but had no answer. "Have to carve up the loot and see."

"And me?"

"I made you a promise. As soon as we reach civilization, you are free to go your own way."

"What if I don't have a way," she said.

My heart pounded in my chest. I had not thought that she would want to remain with me.

Before I could respond a loud roar came from the camp. Several men ran back to where we sat and grabbed rifles. When they fired, a cloud of smoke enveloped us. The beast roared again and I ran toward them. Illuminated by the fire a dark cat's eyes glowed gold and it growled. Its nose twitched, probably from the scent of the powder. It roared again and I could see several cubs behind it. Rivulets of blood were visible on its torso, but it didn't appear to notice. Another round of shots fired and she charged.

I stood frozen in its path, Rory behind me. Weaponless I faced the panther as it charged, noticing it was surprisingly agile for its size. Within seconds, it would be on us, and I knew I must act. More shots fired, and though the beast only paused, I gained enough time to look around. The fire was close and I reached for a long stick, pulled it from the flames and went for the cat. It snarled again and I jabbed it with the stick, unsure if it even noticed it. Again I stuck the glowing tip in her direction, but she shook, tensed her muscles and charged.

The fire was behind me and with no time to move around it, I turned and jumped over it. The flames nicked my legs as I cleared the pit and I felt my leg tear. More shots were fired and I chanced a look behind me. The panther was engulfed in flames with blood spurting from several wounds. I stood in shock; my body just beginning to register the pain from the wounds on my leg from her claws and watched as the cat retreated into the woods.

"After it," I yelled at the men as I collapsed on the ground.

Chapter Two

When I finally woke they said I had been out for three days. The first thing I saw were two eyes staring back and I thought it was the cat over me until I realized it was Lucy. She backed away as if she had seen a ghost, and quickly returned with fresh water. I was stiff and my leg burned, but as I inventoried my body, I found those were my only complaints.

"Mr. Nick, he's awake," she called to the group. "I told you the poison would leave him."

Rory ran to me and took the water from Lucy. The rest of the men stopped what they were doing and followed.

"You've been unconscious for three days, Nick," Rory said. "We thought we lost you."

"Evil beast has poison in its claws," Lucy spoke from behind her.

It came back to me slowly as I drank the offered water and watched the activity around the camp. I scoured my memory for what had happened and slowly pieced the attack together. The last thing I remembered was jumping through the fire. I looked down at my leg, bound in linen from the trader's goods. My toes moved, but I could feel the tightness and burn from the claws.

They had stared long enough and I summoned my voice, "What happened?"

"The panther. Don't you remember?" Rhames emerged through the men.

I was so happy to see him on his feet that I forgot about my own plight. "You're better."

"Aye. The woman is a healer. Look at you. We thought you were gone after the cat took a swipe at your leg. She's been up for three days tending to you."

I looked over at the small woman and noticed her drawn face and the bluish rings under her eyes. "Thank you," I said. My head started to spin and I lay back down. I felt the bristle of the pelt and smelt the musk of recently skinned fur. I had to smile to myself knowing I was lying on the panther's pelt.

It was dark when I woke again. The camp was quiet, a small fire blazing several feet from me. The men had been busy while I had been unconscious. They had created a simple palisades around the perimeter using the brush that surrounded us to keep out any more predators. There was a drying rack above the fire, draped with meat and the ground was littered with simple handmade tools.

Rory must have noticed my movement as I tried to rise, and came toward me.

"Easy there. That leg's a bit nasty."

I grunted as I used her shoulder to gain my feet for the first time in days and tentatively placed a little weight on the injured leg. It held and I started to limp toward the edge of the camp. "Just have to pass some water. I'll be alright," I said over my shoulder to discourage her from following.

"Don't be so proud. I've seen a man pass water before. You need help."

She was not to be denied and allowed me to place an arm over her shoulder. I must not have been too badly hurt as I felt her warmth against me.

"They're uneasy," she whispered.

I looked at the men gathered around the fire and realized they were in two groups watching us. Red, Swift, Johnnie, and Syd were off to one side while Rhames, Blue, and Lucy were together. The split didn't surprise me, but I had no idea what they could want. We had decided on a route and there was no going back to the Indians. For better or worse we were together until we reached open water, or died trying. We went toward the men.

"Now that you've got us in the middle of nowhere you gonna kill us off and take our share?" Red called out.

He must have seen the question on my face.

"Aye, you don't know he took all our guns," he continued and moved closer, the men behind him murmured in approval and followed.

"They was shooting at fairies," Rhames said. "Had to take them away. I think the cat put the fear in them. If they kept that up we'd be out of powder and shot."

While I agreed with his actions, I knew we had to give the guns back. We would need whatever skills each man had in order to escape the river of grass. "You can have them back. But, only enough shot and powder for hunting."

They nodded their heads in approval and I could hear Rhames shifting behind me. "We've got to trust them," I said under my breath. My leg felt like it was about to collapse and I felt Rory grip me tighter. "I trust you haven't wasted the last few days. We leave in the morning."

"Now *that's* the captain talking," Red said and the men agreed.

Rory helped me back to the pelt and Lucy hovered over me, immediately removing the bandage from my leg.

"No move, Mr. Nick," she said.

"She's right. You can't travel like that," Rory said.

"We don't have a choice," I met theirs eyes as I said it. "We'll be in boats. I don't need the leg to paddle."

"You heard the captain. We shove off at first light," Rhames reinforced the order.

The men scattered and Rory and Rhames huddled by me. "What do we have for supplies?" I asked.

"The meat from the cat was rancid, but the boys have shot a few deer and the women have been foraging. Probably enough food for a week or so," he recalled our inventory.

"Well, water is not a problem," I was optimistic that we could reach the Keys in a week. There should be opportunities to hunt along the way, but I felt better knowing we were setting out well provisioned.

"And ammunition?"

"Damned fools wasted more than I want to tell you, but if we don't have to skirmish, we should have enough to hunt."

I jumped as Lucy put a fresh poultice on my wound. As she cleaned the puss, I glanced down at my leg and saw the incisions made by the panther's claws.

"Lucy says the claws have poison. You're lucky she's here," Rory said.

"And Blue as well. Grabbed those claws and boiled them down, he did. After he puts that paste on those darts he blows there won't be a man standing.

***

My leg throbbed, keeping me awake through the night and I wished for the unconscious state I had spent the last few days in. Unable to sleep, I crept closer to the fire and removed the map from its oilskin case. The light reflected off the old parchment and I studied the unknown area. Provided we could take a direct route, the distance seemed close to what we had covered on the lake. I expected it might take longer because of the sawgrass, but as long as there was water underneath it, we could use the poles to push the shallow draft canoes through it.

I must have dozed as movement in the camp startled me awake and I pulled the map away from the edge of the fire where I had dropped it only inches from destruction. Not that it was much help anymore, the area we were about to enter was totally undefined, but all the same, I felt better having it. I placed it back in the oilskin and grabbed the rifle by my side to use as a crutch.

Rhames caught me as I stumbled and hauled me to my feet. "No good to have the men see you like this. Let's get you to the boats. I gained my footing and once standing I was able to use the rifle as a crutch and hobbled to the canoes. I sat on the gunwale of the closest boat and waited for the group to gather. They were ready in minutes and loaded the boats, careful to distribute the treasure and provisions equally, both for weight and to minimize our losses if a boat went down.

I was in the first boat and we were able to use the homemade paddles on the last stretch of open water. After a mile we started to see growth below the water and before we had reached another mile we were in the sawgrass. We stowed the oars and unlashed the poles. I felt guilty having to stay seated as Rhames poled our boat. The craft seemed stable, buffeted by the grass on all quarters. While he pushed us along, I tried to gauge the effort required to move through the stiff vegetation, but his face was unreadable. The grass was everywhere, dark green with some brown and sharp edges which appeared to give it strength. From my position in the hull, I could see little else. With nothing else to look at, I studied the field stretched out in front of us and noticed that the water must be low. There were clear delineations on the blades of sawgrass, similar to the tide markings on the mangroves by the ocean. I looked back at Rhames and watched him as the pole entered and left the water. The bottom appeared to be only a few feet below the boat.

Just as I realized how low the water was, we bumped against a mud shoal. He drove the pole deeper into the muck and the boat moved over it, but I wondered what that small bump foretold of the journey ahead. The next few hours passed without incident and I started to relax and eventually drifted off to sleep.

I was jarred awake as the boat grounded and I felt Rhames jump out. I looked up and saw an island with several small cypress trees, the high water mark on their trunks suggesting that the land would be covered during high water. In this case the low water was a blessing as we had solid land to make camp.

Chapter Three

We ate dried deer meat and drank the juice from the last of the coconuts before savoring the fat-rich meat which we used our hands to scoop from the shells into our mouths. The last day and a half we had poled the boats through never ending fields of sawgrass. Single herons and clouds of small white birds called ibis flew overhead and fish jumped in the small patches of open water. But, for the most part it had been miles of the same, the silence broken only by faraway grunts from the ever present gators. Close to exhaustion, we took turns poling and resting. I tried to gauge our progress, but with no landmarks it was impossible.

As the sun set I tried to take a turn at the pole. Several of the others switched out with Rhames to take a turn in my boat, who had been stoic, as usual, in his efforts. Rory was in the bow of my canoe, leaning against a chest when I rose. The pain in my leg was unbearable for the first few minutes as the blood revisited the wound, but it eased and soon I was used to it. The exercise felt good, although I was terrified we would hit a mud shoal and I would be unable to balance myself. Within minutes, I could see Rory's chest rise and fall in a deep sleep.

It was close to dusk now when I swatted the first mosquito from my nose, hoping it was a stray. The air seemed to get heavier and envelope me in its grasp and I started to sweat. Mosquitos swarmed and I felt feverish. I was about to sit and wake Rory when I felt the first hint of a breeze on my face.

In itself it was nothing, but I turned and looked behind me and saw the moon reveal a long thin line of clouds on the horizon. These winter storms pushed the humidity in front of them, making it feel like dog days of summer, far different than the drier January air, before they moved through. From the looks of it, we were in for a blow, and in the middle of miles of nothing, there was no way to protect ourselves.

"Hurry. Get the boats together." Rory stirred in the bow.

"What's the matter? Can't a girl sleep around here?"

I ignored her and waved the other boats over. "Come on," I called again.

Rhames, Syd, and Blue manned the helms of the other boats, all slightly ahead of ours. They stopped, looked back and waited as I used my good leg to brace myself in order to push harder. I reached them and we lashed the boats together, using our poles as anchors.

With the boats moored as they were, we were closer than we were used to. Most of our previous camps had been large enough we could spread out into groups and get some space, but here we were on top of each other. I noticed the smell of the men, at first unbearable, was no longer there. I glanced back toward the north, where I felt the breeze stiffen.

"I see it too, Mr. Nick," Blue echoed my thoughts.

"It's moving fast," I said as the wind picked up.

The rest of the group noticed our concern.

"We're pretty exposed out here," I said.

I saw Rhames rise in his boat and sniff the air. "Reckon the best thing to do is stay together. There's no cover for miles if there is any at all. We're going to have to ride it out."

What he said made sense. Lashed together we were heavy and stable. By themselves the individual boats could capsize in a big wind. I doubted there would be any waves in this kind of water; the sawgrass sticking through every few inches would buffer any build up. I turned again to the wind and realized that we could use the storm to our favor. The rain would surely raise the level of the water, allowing us to coast over the mud shoals we were constantly fighting and the wind from the north would push us south, toward the Keys.

"Pull the poles," I yelled over the building wind. "Check the lashings and make sure the boats are tied together." In minutes we were floating freely. A loud boom filled the night and an intense light flashed across the sky. The wind picked up another notch as the thunder rolled.

I felt Rory brush against me and looked at her face. A crease formed above her brow, and although it was not panic, there was a glimmer of fear in her eyes.

"What is it?" I asked. She had been as strong as any man so far.

"It's nothing," she turned away. "Just a storm like this one was what put us in your sights."

I remembered the day. A strong winter front had blown through, but we were protected by our island. At first light we could see a large merchant ship, main mast down and leaning over the transom, its sails draped in the water. It was easy prey and we took the ship and its cargo without bloodshed.

"We're safe as long as we stay together," I tried to reassure her and felt her skin brush against mine as she moved closer. Another blast of thunder and flash of lightning, this time so vivid we could see each vein as it pierced the night sky. The first drops of rain fell fat on our faces and we huddled together in the boat. Under normal circumstances I would have been delighted by her closeness, but as the wind started to roar, I feared for our lives.

It was impossible to navigate as the line of clouds passed over heads and blocked the moon. We were destined to go where the storm took us and held onto the gunnels as the wind pushed us through the sawgrass. Lightning flashed and I thought I saw it strike in the distance. Minutes later it struck again and I could see what looked like the glow of a fire on the horizon. The flames grew higher as the wind howled. Suddenly the storm was upon us and rain started to fall in earnest. Driven by the wind it came in sheets, blocking all visibility.

"Bail the boats," I yelled into the wind. Rory must have heard me as she reached for an empty coconut shell and started scooping the water that had already accumulated in the bottom of the canoe.

"We can't stay out here in this," she called back to me.

I had been wrong about the sawgrass stopping the wind from forming waves. Small whitecaps were illuminated with every lightning strike and the raft of boats bounced wildly in the chop. If we hadn't lashed the boats together, I feared we would have capsized by now. "Where the lightning struck. Did you see the fire?"

"Yes, but …."

"It must be land." I didn't wait for an answer but took one of our paddles and used it as a rudder to steer the raft of boats in the direction I had seen the blaze. I did my best to hold course, but the blade was too small and the bulk of the boats too much. Rhames must have seen my attempt because he joined me.

All night the storm blew and we each took turns steering. By daybreak we were tired and waterlogged. There had been no rest as the rain accumulated in the boats and whoever was not at the helm was forced to bail. The sun, still below the horizon, turned the sky a deep red to our left and I was at least reassured we were still headed in the right direction. As it rose, the red faded and the orange orb floated into a deep blue sky. It was cooler now, but at least the wind and rain had stopped. We were moving fast as well, the water seeming to have some current to it and soon I spotted a lone dead tree on a spit of sand.

"Land," I yelled as if we had been at sea for months. A half hour later we unlashed the boats when we were within a few yards of the shore and each poled our craft to the beach.

I was the last ashore and watched as the group collapsed on the ground exhausted. As I stepped over the gunwale I felt my leg give out and found myself face down in the water. Blue and Lucy ran to my aid and hauled me to the beach where the others gathered round me. It must have been the adrenaline from the storm wearing off because I had felt no pain all night, but now it was back and as harsh as I could imagine. They rolled my pants leg up and I saw a few men look away at the sight of the claw marks. Red and swollen, the four lines looked like they were about to burst.

"Start a fire," Lucy called to Blue. "He'll be alright. Just been too long without medicine," she reassured the group. "We must stay here until he heals."

Chapter Four

From the height of the sun in the sky, I figured it was early in the afternoon when I woke. I looked down at my leg and saw only the linen wrapping. The crippling pain was gone, replaced with a dull burning.

"You going to help out around here, or do I have to pull your weight as well," Rory walked up to me.

I was about to respond when I saw the smile on her face and remembered the closeness we had shared in the storm. "Aye. Might need you for a while," I said.

"Lucy says we need to stay here for a few days. You should be healed enough to travel by then." She carried something dark in a palmetto leaf and set it down beside me.

I looked warily at what appeared to be fresh charcoal from the tree. "What are you doing with that? And where's Lucy?"

The smile was gone, "She's gone fishing with Blue. It's my turn to watch you or I'd be with them as well instead of playing nursemaid."

She kneeled down next to me and removed the linen. I tensed, preparing for the pain as the fabric released from the open cuts. The wound looked better, but the claw marks were still open and swollen. A bowl of what looked like water sat next to her and she mixed the charcoal into the liquid and stirred it with a branch. When it had dissolved she used the linen and washed the wound with it. "Lucy says this will take the evil from it. Me, I'd leave it in you. You could use some toughening up."

I shrank from her comment, but she smiled again. "How long did she say?"

"Probably two days and it'll scab over." She continued washing the wound, digging a little deeper each time to clean out the cuts. "It's not a bad thing really. The group is as relaxed as we've been since you rescued me. There's plenty of food and a little rest won't hurt."

She was right, but I was impatient. We might have felt safe, but I was apprehensive about the unknown, uncharted waters surrounding us. In my view, the sooner we left this river of grass and entered the open water of the Keys, the better, but I kept my feelings to myself.

We sat next to each other, talking about our individual struggles for freedom among the pirates when we heard a scream. I got to my feet and followed her. When we got to the beach, Syd was a hundred feet out, a pole stuck in the mud, neck deep in the water. He must have been trying to spear a fish and stepped into a soft spot.

Red and Swift were first into the water to help Syd. I limped over, stood behind Rory and watched them sink into the silt as well. With every movement they further entangled themselves in the muddy loam. The water soon turned brown as centuries of rotting vegetation floated to the surface.

"Johnnie and Blue, take a boat to them," I yelled. Rhames glanced back at me as if his name should have been called, but I was still suspect of his health. We would talk later. The two men grabbed an empty canoe and poled toward the victims. Syd was chest deep in the muck and sinking further with every movement. We yelled for him to be still, but he was in a panic and continued trying to extricate himself. Swift was halfway to him and now trapped in knee-deep muck.

The boat pulled alongside Syd and he grabbed the gunwale and started to pull. "Rest your body on the boat and let them pull you out," I yelled. "Take it slow," I cautioned aware of the instability of the narrow canoe. The last thing we needed was two more men trapped in the water. Bubbles started to surface around Syd as they pulled and his body started to slide free. Another minute and he was in the boat, collapsed on the deck.

I heard a loud grunt and turned to Swift. The noise repeated itself and echoed several times, but I was focused on the rescue and ignored it. Syd was back on shore and the canoe moved toward the next man.

"Is the gators, Mr. Nick," Blue called to me as the grunts continued. I looked around but saw no sign of the beasts and turned my focus back to Swift. Having watched Syd's rescue, Swift was calm and soon aboard the boat. While this had been going on, Rhames and Rory had used two poles and pulled Red onto dry land.

We were back on the beach when we all turned to the loudest grunt yet. This time I saw the eyes of the gator and followed the ridges on his back that jutted out of the water all the way to his tail, a good dozen feet away. He raised his snout and grunted again, another chorus echoed back. His tail swept from side to side and we stood in place as he walked onto the beach.

"Get the guns," I yelled to the group. While they ran to the boats to retrieve the firearms, I scanned the shores of our small island and noticed that we were surrounded. "The boats. Get into the boats," I yelled hoping they would provide some protection from the attack that looked eminent. I limped over to the closest canoe, sat on the gunwale and got into the hull as I watched the others do the same. Rifle barrels were pointed in all directions and I couldn't help but notice we were in each others' line of fire.

Eyes emerged in pairs from the water and I realized that the commotion caused by the trapped men had alerted the animals to our presence. They were everywhere. "On my order," I called out and the men's attention focused on my voice. "Guns to the south and fire," I yelled.

A blast, loud enough to cause my ears to ring echoed from the boats and smoke filled the air. Several guns fired a minute later after reloading and I called for them to cease fire. We didn't have enough ammunition to fire aimlessly. What we needed was to clear a passage and escape. Blue blew through his tube, shooting projectiles at the creatures, but their thick skin turned the darts away.

"Turn to the east and fire," I ordered with the same result. We repeated the exercise to the west and I waited for the smoke to clear.

Carcasses lay on the shores and unfazed by our actions, more creatures were climbing over them. Several started to eat their own dead, but still they came. I had the men fire the same pattern again and before waiting for the outcome had them jump from the boats and push them into the water. Someone screamed, but I couldn't see who as I was on the far side of the group.

"Aim toward the water. We need to clear a path and get out of here. They won't be a threat once we're on the water." I could only hope this was true, fearing that with one strong stroke of its tail, a beast of this size could easily capsize our overloaded and top-heavy craft.

The rifles fired again and we pushed the canoes the last few feet toward the water, careful not to step into the mud. As one, we were in the crafts and pushing away from land. I watched the scene on shore as Rory poled our boat. Most of the gators were on the beach now, feasting on the dead animals when I noticed the shape of a man amongst them. He was muddy and missing several limbs. I scanned our group and noticed Syd alone in his boat. Another look around confirmed it was Johnnie.

The rest of the group realized what was happening and we sat still in the water watching the slaughter with horror on our faces. We had seen enough blood and gore in our time for several lives, but I don't think any of us had ever witnessed a scene like this one. The frenzy continued with many of the beasts engaged in deadly battles, unable to curb their bloodlust.

"He's gone," I called meekly, feeling responsible for Johnnie's demise. "We've got to get out of here before they regroup." Each of us took one last look at the island and turned grimly back to the endless expanse of sawgrass ahead.

Without a word we poled non-stop until dark our only guide the setting sun which we kept on our right. In the fading light I tried to find a place to camp, but although several of the boats had hit bottom when we first started out, there was no solid land in sight. I feared the water was rising, pouring from the lake and slowly covering the dry land. Finally as darkness enveloped us I called for a halt.

We brought the canoes together and planted the poles vertically in the muck, then lashed the boats to them. Still silent, we moved around our crafts trying to get comfortable for the night ahead.

Chapter Five

By the height of the moon in the sky, I could guess it was about midnight when we gave up our makeshift camp to the mosquitos. The swarming bugs attracted by our unbathed bodies made it impossible to sleep. The incessant buzzing of the bugs and the grunts of the gators after our close call and the loss of Johnnie unnerved us. Silently, we separated the canoes, pulled the poles from the muck and started to float into the night. My leg ached, but I struggled to take the first turn at the pole, using a distant star to track our course.

I assigned two-hour shifts and we took turns at the helm through the night using the stars to navigate. Despite the discomfort of the canoe, I slept fitfully during Rory's last watch and woke with the sun. The landscape had changed overnight. Mangrove islands were visible in the distance and I sensed the water flow had increased. I scooped water with one hand and brought it to my mouth. To my disdain and relief, it was brackish; the fresh water diluted with salt from the incoming tide. My relief was that we were close to the coast, but my worry was that we were out of fresh water and could no longer rely on the miles of fresh water that had been around us.

I took the pole and checked our course against the position of the sun. My mouth was dry, but I continued in silence, knowing the others suffered the same fate. In the distance I could see clouds and my first thought was rain. During the summer these clouds would blossom into anvil-based thunderheads, but this time of year I thought it might be a land mass they were attracted to. The mangrove islands on either side of us became closer and denser as we floated by them and I felt the water change beneath us. Another hour and we were in a seam, like you find in a river, that turned us to the west. The channel was deep and clearly delineated now that the sawgrass was gone and soon we had to lash the poles to the boats and use our paddles.

The mood lightened as the channel opened to reveal an expanse of islands in the distance. At first I was jubilant, but as I continued to monitor the river's western course, I started to worry. Gasparilla had travelled the route from the Keys up the west coast of Florida and this area looked familiar. I glanced at Rhames who would have noticed as well, but he was laid out and resting, his face toward the sky. I would have to wait until he finished his shift paddling to confirm my suspicion. For now I would keep quiet. If I was in fact correct, we were in the Shark River, a tidal basin that emptied into the Gulf of Mexico, miles of open water away from the protection of the Keys.

I allowed the group to revel in the accomplishment of our escape from the river of grass and kept my thoughts to myself. After all, we could well be the first white men to make the journey. If there were others before us, I hadn't heard their claims. Rory took over at the helm and I sat in the bow studying the islands in the distance. The water had taken a light green color and along the mangroves I could see fish rolling and jumping. My thoughts were broken by a strange site on the horizon. Two small vertical lines appeared over an island not too far in the distance. They were too straight to belong in nature and as we closed, I whispered to Rory to pole toward the far bank.

We formed a semicircle with our backs to the mangroves. The group turned toward me as I looked back at the open water. I whispered in case my voice carried over the water, "Right then, we've gotten out of one pot and climbed into another."

All but Rhames looked confused. He nodded in agreement.

"It's the Shark River we're in. The Captain's had us take refuge here before. That's the good news. The river of grass is behind us, but the worst of it is that these boats will do us little good out there." They followed my gaze to the west. Several fingers pointed at the top of the masts I had seen earlier. "That's right. Back to pirating, but this time it not for the loot but for our own survival. We need that boat if we are going any further.

Rory looked distraught. "Why don't you just pay them off? There's a fortune in the chests."

The men looked at her with odd looks on their faces. "We don't know who they are. Holed up in the river, they could be pirates, slavers or both," I said.

She looked down. "I'm just sayin' we could see what they're about before you bloody lot go and murder them."

"Right then," I said. My plan was to scout them out anyway. If that kept her happy and quiet, all the better. I organized the group and appointed Red leader while Rhames, Blue, and I took the biggest boat, unloaded the chest onto another canoe to make our craft lighter and faster should we need to make a quick escape. I took Rhames for his knowledge and Blue for his instincts, desperately hoping between the two mens' skill sets that we could form a plan to take the boat. We stayed against the shore as we made our way toward the open water. Rhames, the strongest, paddled and Blue sat forward, forgoing his blow tube for a rifle. I sat in the stern, feeling useless, but even the easy maneuver to switch boats had caused my leg to revolt in pain.

I lost sight of the masts as we crossed to the island where we beached the boat and I worried that they had raised anchor and left, until I heard the talk of men through the brush. I stayed with the craft, a rifle ready, while Rhames and Blue went inland. Minutes later they emerged and silently crept back into the canoe. I was already at the oars, ready to move when Rhames signaled me to move out. The boat was silent until we were across the river and out of earshot.

"It's a schooner - merchant from the look of her. Less than a dozen men," Rhames said. "From the looks of it, they had some trouble in the storm and sought refuge here."

"Can we take it?"

"Aye, anything can be taken," he grinned clearly healed and back in his element. "But we need to act fast. From the looks of them, they'll be leaving on the outgoing tide this afternoon," he said.

My mind was working trying to calculate the odds. We were half their manpower if Rhames had judged correctly, and I suspected he had. A pitched fight would surely result in casualties to our side which we could not afford. "We're gonna have to sneak up on them."

"Aye," He looked at Blue who grinned. "While you were sleeping, we made some of those devil tubes like he's got." With the poison from the cat's claws and you three taking shots, we should be able to knock out at least half and make it a fair fight."

I nodded acceptance, upset about being relegated to light duty, but with my leg as it was, I had little choice. I couldn't help but notice the tide, slack on our way out, was now starting to ebb. We would have to act now. The group gathered around as Rhames outlined his plan. Lucy, Blue, Rory, and I would take a canoe and go back to the spot we had just landed, make our way across the island and wait for the men to approach. In typical pirate treachery Rhames and the other men would load themselves into one canoe and approach the boat as if they were being chased by Indians. The men on the merchant ship would hardly expect an attack from inland and they would go to the rail, more out of curiosity than suspect, to see what was going on. From that point, we would have a clear view of their backs.

The men began loading the chests in the two remaining boats and secured them to the mangrove branches. We left before them, retracing the route we had just used. As I rowed, I couldn't help but notice the look on Rory's face.

"What is it?"

"I thought you were going to scout it out and offer them pay?" she said.

I hesitated.

"Pirates is what it is," she hissed. "I want no part of this. You swore to drop me off at the first sign of civilization and I'm calling you on it now. Leave these men be and let me go."

I continued rowing, wanting to respect my oath, but I had to consider the others as well. Fortunately I was saved from the decision by Lucy who withdrew a dart and went for Rory's neck.

The boat swayed and almost capsized as I lunged to stop her, forcing the dart to land in her arm instead. Rory fell over instantly.

"You killed her," I tried to keep my voice down.

"No, Mr. Nick. You saved her. If it would've gone into her neck, yes I would have killed her, but in that part of the arm, she'll sleep for a bit," she smiled as if this had been her plan all along.

Blue took over and focused our attention on the task at hand.

My heart was pounding in my chest when we reached the shore and the adrenaline coursing through my blood that one feels before battle, dimmed the pain in my leg to the point where I hardly noticed it when I got out of the boat. I looked behind at Rory, head down on her chest and slumped against a gunwale and decided that she wouldn't have to worry about being a pirate after all if she slept through the whole pirating thing. We left her there and crept through the mangroves.

The canoe was in sight when we reached the beach on the seaward side of the island and waited behind the last copse of mangroves. The men on the merchant ship were gathering at the rail as the men in the approaching canoe yelled and waved for help. As they approached, I watched Lucy and Blue swing the tubes from their backs and stick several darts in the sand. I followed their lead and readied myself.

The men were distracted by the approaching canoe and I reached down, stuck a dart in the tube and put it to my mouth. Before I could aim and blow, I noticed the two Africans in a blur of activity besides me. As I looked up to aim, I saw two men drop. Before I had blown once, they had already fired two darts each. With a third about to follow, I inhaled through my nose and blew as hard as I could. I don't know if it was my shot, or if they had gotten off two more, but two more men dropped to the deck of the boat. As we reloaded and fired again I heard the sound of several rifles fire. Smoke enveloped the ship and canoe now, and I couldn't tell who had fired or what the result was.

Chapter Six

I waited impatiently knowing there was nothing to be done until the smoke cleared. Once it did I was relieved to see it was our men who had fired. It looked like two more men were down and we had yet to lose anyone. Lucy fired another dart while I reloaded. Blue was in the open now, calculating that the men onboard the boat were focused on the attack from the canoe and had not yet realized the danger at their backs.

He fired again, and another man fell. Lucy and I came out next to him and watched the fight as our men fired another round. I realized they were stuck with no means to board the ship. It was up to us to create a diversion to allow them time.

The crew on the boat was fixated on the men in the canoe, both groups firing on each other. I saw the anchor line as a means to surprise them. With a hand signal for Blue and Lucy to follow, I moved into the water and started to swim toward the bow of the boat. Once I reached the chain, I took the tail of my shirt to protect my hands, swung my legs above me and started to climb upside down. My leg resisted every movement, but in this position, I could use three limbs and brace with the bad leg. I reached the deck and hand over hand, hauled myself forward. Blue and Lucy were behind me and we searched for cover.

We huddled behind the foremast, impatient, but knowing we needed the element of surprise. They had not realized what the small darts were or where they had come from and we readied to shoot again. This time I called out to get their attention and as soon as they turned we blew, taking three more men to the deck. The rest charged and we pulled our knives hoping we had given Rhames and the men enough time to climb to the deck. The war cries distracted the crew from attacking us and they turned again to see Rhames, Syd, Swift, and Red, cutlasses drawn behind them.

The sides were evenly matched and I noticed trickles of blood flowing from wounds on Syd and Red. The men clashed and I could detect no weakness from their injuries. The fight moved toward us as Rhames and the other men pushed the merchants back. I glanced down at the knife in my hand. Lucy and Blue were ready as well and although they were not the heavier blades the other men were fighting with, we would attack from behind. It was time to enter the fray. I nodded at the couple and crept away from cover. Unobserved, I crept to within a few feet of the fight, took a gulp of air and leaped forward.

One man saw me and turned, but the moment of indecision cost him his life as the hesitation gave Rhames an unobstructed cut with his sword. There were only three of them standing now and each dropped his weapon and dove into the water.

A part of me always was revolted by what happened next, but if you choose pirating for your career, you have to suffer some of the unpleasantness. I could only watch as Rhames and the other men went to the rail and started firing into the water.

Blood stains soon clouded the water and after a few more shots, they looked at each other and let loose a primal scream of victory. I put the image of the men being picked off out of my mind and went to check on our crew.

"Rhames, you and Swift go back for the treasure. Blue, go and get Rory." I turned to Syd and Red and offered assistance to Lucy who was already tending their wounds.

The adrenaline left as fast as it had come and I found myself standing in a pool of a dead man's blood unable to move. The wound on my calf reminded me it was still there as I limped toward the rail, leaned against the gunwale and surveyed the deck. Men lay scattered and the worn oak deck had a red tint to it. Syd moved toward me, his arm wrapped in linen.

"You alright?"

"Could have been worse," he said

"Think we can haul the meat over the side?"

"The sooner the better," he said and went to the first body.

I let go of the rail and tested my leg before going to aid him. It was no worse for the action, and together we slid the first body over the side. I looked up after it splashed and saw the canoe with Blue and Lucy make the turn around the island and head for the boat. Rory was still unconscious and I hoped she would remain that way until we could clean up this mess, load the treasure, and get underway. Syd and I tossed the remaining bodies into the water and Red came to help as we used several buckets to start washing the blood off the deck.

I left Syd and Red to the work and went to the transom where Blue was holding the canoe against the larger ship while Lucy climbed the rope ladder.

"We gonna need some help, Mr. Nick," he called up.

I looked around and saw a block and tackle hanging from a boom with a rope fed through the pulley leading into a hold. The rope came free with a pull and I retrieved its end, limped back to the transom and tossed it to the boat. Blue grabbed the end and made a harness around Rory's waist. When he signaled he was ready, I called Red and

Syd over and together we hauled on the rope. The block and tackle creaked under the load, but her limp body was soon aboard.

"Take her below and find a cabin she can be comfortable in," I turned to Lucy, "How much longer is she going to be out?"

"No telling how deep the dart went. Could be minutes, could be hours."

Hours would find us well into the Gulf with a clean ship, but minutes would allow her to witness the remnants of the fight. I wanted to tell her we had left the men the canoes, not that they had been murdered in cold blood. "Lock the door," I called to the men as they grabbed her under the arms and hauled her down the passageway. It was the last thing I wanted to do, but I could not bear her judgement if she saw what had happened.

Once she was out of sight I turned to the horizon and saw the canoes laden with treasure, the boats riding low in the water, coming toward us. Can you stay there and rig the chests."

The two canoes pulled alongside and we started to haul the chests aboard. Red and Syd struggled, but they weighed more than Rory and I was braced against the rail, unable to help as I guided the line away from the boat to keep it from breaking. We waited while Rhames and Swift climbed a rope ladder and between the four men onboard and Blue rigging from the boats, the chests were quickly lifted and set in the hold below.

I had gone below to guide the chests into place and untie them. With the last chest secured, I looked around the dark hold and saw bails of tobacco, barrels of spices and crates with no markings. It wasn't a huge sum, but it would delay the need to spend the treasure once we got to port. I was still wary of using the silver, gold, and gems as an explanation would almost certainly be required of where they came from. There was still room in the hold, the chests, for all their value took up little space.

I climbed the ladder and yelled to Rhames, "Rig a canoe. There is enough room for two in the hold."

He gave me one of his queer looks, but tossed the rope down to Blue and called out instructions. We had been through the shallow waters of the Keys several times and I knew their danger. The Gulf to the north of the chain of islands was dangerous and the shallow draft boats would be useful. It took all the men to get the boats in and there was little room, once they were stowed, but I felt better for having them.

My leg was close to spent as I climbed out of the hold into the waning light. Red and Syd had done a good job washing down the decks and only a careful examination would reveal the slaughter that had taken place not two hours ago.

"Rhames. Take her out," I relinquished command to the more experienced sailor.

He issued orders and the boat was soon pointed to open water, the onshore breeze and ebb tide working her out of the mouth of the river. While he got the boat underway, I found the captain's cabin and started examining the papers and charts scattered on the small desk and bed. From a cursory look, the ship was headed to New Orleans, but the manifest showed no goods. It appeared we had encountered smugglers. The quick read of the log showed the ship departing Havana ten days ago, staying in deeper water past the Keys and seeking refuge in the river when the storm hit. Their route suited my next move. Had they stopped over in the Keys, I would have been forced to choose another destination as the boat and crew would have been know.

Just as I finished I heard a banging on the door adjacent to mine and I braced myself for the fight to come. There was no point in delay, which would just anger her further, so I left the cabin and went to the locked door.

Chapter Seven

Glass crashed against the door as I opened it and peered through the small crack, but I couldn't see her through the small opening. Suddenly the door flew open and I took a blow to the head. I staggered back, but she pulled me into the room.

"Pirates. The lot of you," she screamed. "Don't even lie to me. I know you killed the crew."

I hadn't yet decided if I was going to lie to her on not, but there was no denying it. I remembered some advice from the captain and held my tongue. He had always said that when a storm hits, the best thing to do is hold tight and let it blow out. I braced myself for the next assault.

Her face was red and I could see her chest heave as she tried to control her breathing. I moved to the side of the doorway seeking the comfort of the wall behind me and hoping I could escape through the door at my side if I needed.

"Damn it Nick. I was just starting to like you."

Her comment hurt worse than another blow. "But…."

"But, nothing. If you're the captain, then captain. You've got a fortune in those chests. Surely you could have bought passage for us."

Again her comments stung. Pirating was ingrained in us, but I had considered our options before choosing to attack. Instead I shifted the blame to the men, "It was bloodlust. They don't know any other way."

"They may not, but I know you do."

I waited for more, but the color in her face had returned to normal. "What's done is done," I said for lack of words. "Now what?"

"Now you're going to leave my cabin and drop me at the next port."

I slid sideways and backed out of the door, closing it behind me. In the passageway I breathed deeply and climbed the ladder to the main deck. The air felt good on my face and I watched the water as it passed under our keel. We were heading southwest seeking deeper water before we would turn south. I rubbed the knot on my head and tried to put the conversation with Rory from my mind, except the words: *I was just starting to like you*, rang in my head. There were tasks to be done. I needed to check our supplies and course, but I was frozen by the rail, staring out to sea, stuck in despair.

A call from the helm snapped me out of my mood and I climbed the short flight of stairs to the wheel. Rhames held the spokes, turning the wheel to correct course and keep the sails full. "What's our course?"

"That's better. You be needin' to get on with it."

I took the scolding, knowing I deserved it. "Course?" I repeated the question.

"Southwest. The wind is backing us and we're in deeper water now."

"Good." I looked over the side at the color of the water, a deep blue now. Both masts of the had their main and topsails unfurled.

Attached to the bowsprit were three triangular shaped jibs. It was a fast boat and I went to the helm where I found the log line used to gauge speed and tossed it over the side letting the progress of the boat pull the triangle-shaped board tied to the end line. I counted the seconds in my head. After a count of thirty, I stopped the line and retrieved it counting the knots as the line came aboard. "Six and a bit," I called to Rhames. The number of knots indicated our speed. I examined the rigging and checked the set of the sails. The wind was fresh on my face with a fair breeze.

"Six and a half knots in a fair breeze," I repeated. "Not bad for this design."

A rare smile crossed his face, "Aye. She handles well."

"We need to make port at Cayo Hueso, drop the girl and get provisions."

"Aye, that one's nothing but trouble."

"Right." I had to agree, but couldn't get her out of my mind. The image of her standing before me red-faced and chest heaving had excited me.

"I can set a course and watch schedule if you like," he said. "Maybe some rum for the rest."

I looked around the deck at the men. Half a dozen were against the rail talking.

"No rum until we make port and drop the girl." I knew it would be unpopular, but we needed our wits about us. For all our travels, we were less than a hundred miles from Gasparilla Island where our journey had started, and the chance of running into a Navy patrol was good. "We draw about half a dozen feet from the looks of her. Set a course more to the south and start dropping the lead every few minutes." I said figuring we would be safer skirting the shallower waters near land. "Keep her to at least three fathoms."

I left him without waiting for an answer. It was his job to set the watch and navigate from here. I went below to the captain's cabin and laid out on the bed. My leg began to throb, but despite the pain, I didn't wake until the sun hit my face through the small port hole.

My first thought was for the boat and I jumped off the bed, still fully dressed and landed on my bad leg. Pain shot through me, but I gritted my teeth and it took my weight. First I would attend to the matters aboard the ship and then I would seek out Lucy and ask her to have a look. I left the cabin and climbed the short ladder to the deck where the wind greeted me. It had picked up overnight and I felt the boat beneath my feet creak as it plowed through the small whitecaps visible over the rail. I held the guardrail and climbed to the helm.

Red was at the wheel. "Course, speed, and depth," I rattled off the questions knowing he would expect them and be prepared with answers.

"Morning to you as well. Bearing due west at seven knots. Water below us is steady at three and a half fathoms."

I ignored the jibe and concentrated on our situation. "How long ago did we change course?"

"Before my watch. I took over from Swift and he said Rhames had changed it an hour before that."

Three hours would put us close to twenty miles closer to land and I looked over the bow to see if any was visible. I had an idea where Rhames would have changed course and estimated we could expect to site some of the smaller outer Keys soon. I was distracted from my calculations as Rory came on deck and I braced myself for the storm sure to follow.

She was calmer this morning, apparently having accepted her fate, or maybe just biding her time until she was free of us. A thought had been on my mind since our conversation last night.

"Let's go forward where we can talk without being overheard," I grabbed her arm and led her to the bow. She resisted slightly, but I wanted the crew to see that I had a handle on her.

"Let go."

"I'm not hurting you and it's for show," I whispered.

We sat on the cover of the forward hold, both looking intently ahead, hoping for the first glimpse of land which meant different things to each of us. "We've got a problem," I began.

She looked at me. "You have problems. I am getting off this boat and away from you murderers."

"That is the problem," I continued before she could interrupt. "You think this band of rogues is going to let you walk away knowing what you know?" She looked at me and I knew I had her attention. "You know about the treasure and the murders. You know the whole story. Do you think you can just walk away from that?"

"The lot of you needs to meet the noose," she said.

"Talk like that's not going to get you home."

"It's the truth."

There was no point in arguing with her. "I intend to honor my agreement with you, but we have to create a ruse or this bunch won't let you out of their sight alive," I continued before she could interrupt. "I have a plan, but you'll need to do your part."

"As long as it has nothing to do with pirating or murder, I'll do as you ask. But," she paused. "Cross me and I'll watch this sorry lot of yours hang. I swear it."

I looked away from her and saw a dot on the horizon. "There's the first island," I pointed. "You can be off this boat tomorrow and have your life back if you play along."

Chapter Eight

The ship came to life as we passed the first small Key. This was a tricky piece of water to navigate; shallow and riddled with shoals. Swift was forward dropping the lead every few minutes and calling back the depth to Rhames who held the wheel. He knew these waters better than any of us, but I could tell by the look on his face he was worried.

"You know how to find the pass?" I approached him.

"Aye, but it a bit tricky in this light. Best around noon when the sun'll show you the deeper water."

I nodded for him to continue.

"You'll be following this chain of islands for sixty miles, then there'll be a gap and if you look to the left, there'll be a chain of small cays curling toward the south. Mind the three-fathom line and turn toward the land in the distance. Follow the angle of the islands and you won't ground."

I was thankful for his knowledge and looked toward the sun now about two hand widths above the horizon and calculated it would be dark in a couple of hours. We still had sixty miles of water between us and the pass leading to Cayo Hueso. Too little time by a long shot to reach the channel and sailing these waters at night was dangerous. The best thing to do would be to anchor here, where we'd be safe for the night, and move on in the morning.

"Let's anchor for the night then. It'd be good for everyone to get a bit of rest. We'll have to set a watch, but just one man at a time."

"Aye," they responded.

We turned to the south and approached the shallow water, a light green in the setting sun. I called to the men to drop sail and allowed the boat to coast to a stop about a hundred yards from a small island. "Drop the hook."

The chain rattled from the forward compartment as the anchor found the bottom and grabbed. The swing of the boat into the current let me know it held. Rhames ordered a hundred more feet of rode to be lowered before he was satisfied. I checked to make sure we were clear of any obstacles as the wind had died and the tide would swing us around when it changed.

"Right then. Let's get some food and set a watch. Tomorrow we make port." I laid out the rotation of two-hour shifts before I left the deck and entered my cabin. I needed to think and wanted to be alone.

Minutes later, my peace was broken as Blue and Lucy approached the door. I called them in and Lucy went to my leg to check the wound. Blue stood nervously by the door and I sensed this was not the reason for their visit.

"You can close it if you want to talk," I said as Lucy removed the bandage. The leg looked close to normal in size and color now, although the claw marks were vivid and would leave a nasty scar.

He shut the door. "Mr. Nick," he started, but stopped as if searching for words.

Lucy took over, "We are scared to go to the big port the others are talking about."

I thought I knew why, but let them continue.

Now that she had broken the ice, Blue started, "We are escaped slaves. If the wrong person should see us, we will be hung, or returned."

I laughed, realizing it was the first time in days. "You're not the only ones that'll be hung if the wrong person sees you. Several of the other crew have been pirating for too long." Their concern made me complete the plan that was already forming in my head. "I was planning on putting them ashore at the island here and setting up a camp. You are welcome to go with them. I am little known and will take a skeleton crew to pilot the boat." I chose not to tell them of Rory's desire to leave, although on a boat this small there were few secrets.

"Thank you, Mr. Nick," Lucy said as they left.

I left the cabin and went on deck where I climbed aloft and looked out at the islands off the port side. There were three and the larger looked to be a few hundred yards around, fair size, but you never knew if the mangroves concealed solid land or swamp. The deep water went to within feet of a small beach. There was a little light left and I called to several of the men sitting on the deck to haul one of the canoes out of the hold.

We rigged the block and tackle to the canoe and with four of us on the line, hauled the craft into the clear, swung it over the side and set it in the water. I wanted to take Rory so I could tell her my plan without the prying ears of the crew, but she wasn't in sight. Instead I decided on Blue. If there was any man amongst us that could judge the habitat, it was him.

We climbed down the rope ladder and dropped into the boat where we each took a paddle and made our way toward the island. We quickly reached the small beach I had seen from the rigging, where we landed. I got out of the canoe, realizing we had gone sans weapons, but there was little threat on this mangrove-covered spit. Blue took the lead as we went to the edge of the brush and entered the interior.

I felt clumsy as I followed him. Where he seemed to navigate the web of palm fronds and mangroves, I stumbled between them. To my surprise, we reached a small clearing near what I expected was the center of the island. It wasn't large, but was high and dry. It appeared to have been used previously, as there remained evidence of a fire ring, fish bones, and stone tools. I picked up a small scraping stone and examined its crude construction. Everything appeared to be ancient, probably left from an Indian band camped here long ago.

"This is a good place," Blue said as he walked the perimeter of the clearing and peered into the brush. "Maybe no water, but the land is solid and there are no bugs."

He was right. I had expected to be assaulted by mosquitos, but now realized there were none. This island seemed to rise from the water, unlike the moist, swamp land the tortuous insects favored. We returned to the beach and paddled the canoe back to the ship just as the sun was about to disappear. I glanced back at the sun, its corner cut off by a palm tree extending toward the water, and felt for the first time in weeks that it was good to be alive. That is until I saw the fiery look on Rory's face as I climbed the ladder and stepped on the deck.

"Why are we anchored and not in port?" she accused.

"Easy girl," I said more confidently than I felt. "It's too late in the day to navigate these waters. We'll pull anchor and be in port tomorrow." She glared at me again and went below.

"Girl's got it for you," Rhames said.

I wasn't sure what he meant and ignored the comment. "The land is arid and there is a clearing toward the center of the island. Tomorrow we can send a group to set up camp there. It'd be a mistake to make port like this." I looked around at the unwashed and dirty group, our clothes torn and bloodstained. He nodded approval and volunteered to be in charge of the shore party, partially I expected, because he was the most notorious of our group.

I went below to check the old crews' stores and see if there were clothes that would fit us when I heard sobbing coming from behind Rory's cabin door. I knocked lightly, half hoping that she would turn me away, but I needed a few minutes with her to explain my plan. To my surprise the door opened.

She was disheveled and wiped her nose on her sleeve. "I expect you have a plan to get me off this boat?"

"I do, but there is some subterfuge involved."

"What else would I expect from you?" She turned away.

I explained my plan and left the cabin, feeling amiss about leaving her. Part of me wanted to stay and comfort her, the other to be far away from her accusations. Before we reached port, I needed to inventory the hold and take some coin for provisions and negotiate a passage for Rory. I grabbed Rhames and asked that he accompany me below. The last thing I needed was to be seen going into the hold alone and arouse the suspicions of the crew.

We took a lantern and climbed the wooden ladder into the hold. I set the lantern down and looked around at the dim and damp space. Our last canoe on top of several bales of tobacco, the treasure chests off to the side. Across the way were several barrels and crates.

"We should take the treasure ashore in case something happens," I said as I went to the chests. "It is high enough to bury it there."

We set the chests below the hold where they could be lifted in the morning. I opened one, reached in, and took out a handful of gold and silver coins. "I'm taking these to buy her way onto another boat," I looked up to see if anyone was in earshot and told him my plan.

Chapter Nine

Pounding on my door woke me the next morning. I rubbed my eyes and focused my attention on my leg, realizing for the first time since the attack it did not hurt. The door opened without my prompting and Rory stood as a silhouette, her hair aflame in rising sun.

"You going to get your pirates moving? Sun's up."

I ignored the barb and looked at the linen wrapping the wound. It came off clean and the scab protecting the cuts was flaking off revealing healthy pink skin beneath it. I left the wound uncovered and rose.

"That looks better."

It was the first personal thing that had come out of her mouth in days. "We'll get to it soon. Got to unload the boat and send some of the crew to the island."

She turned and left without a word. It was curious with her. I know I felt something and was pretty sure she did as well, but as long as she branded us pirates, there was no hope. I hadn't wanted to be a pirate, rather, I had no choice as I was abducted by Gasparilla the same as she. Fortune just had it that I was a boy - and able to read. I heard activity on the deck and left my past in the cabin as I climbed to the deck.

The sun was out and the men were all up. Rhames had started moving the chests to the island and I watched as the men heaved the last of them onto the deck. I sat and watched them finish the work and said a quick goodbye to Rhames as he and Red disappeared down the rope ladder. Lucy and Blue had already gone ashore, leaving me with Swift, Syd, and Rory.

I gathered the group together and we watched the canoe disappear around the island in the direction of the beach. "Right then. You and Syd work the sails. Rory will be at the helm and I will navigate and work the lead." I checked the morning breeze before determining how much canvas to put out, then looked north to where I expected the three-fathom line was to decide on our heading. It would be a mistake in these shallow waters to pull the anchor without a clear course.

"We'll head to deep water and follow the three-fathom line to Cayo Hueso. Set the main," I ordered before moving forward to bring in as much of the anchor rode as I could. Once the boat was directly over the anchor, I tied it off, hoping the movement of the boat would drag it free of the sandy bottom.

"You said Indian Key yesterday and that it would take a few hours," Rory said.

"Change of plans. You've a better chance of getting on a boat at Cayo Hueso. It'll take a bit longer, but the navigation is straight forward." She seemed to accept this and went to the wheel. Swift and Syd pulled on the halyard on the main mast and the large sail rose from the lazy jacks supporting it on the boom. About two thirds of the way up the mast, they tied it off and we waited for it to fill. The wind was from the southeast as it typically is here unless a front blows from the north. The canvas filled and pulled us forward. The boat lurched with only the weight of the anchor holding it back. I moved to the winch with the other men and we put our backs into it. The anchor came aboard easily with the three of us and once stowed, I went to the helm and took the lead line from the navigation station.

"Steer us straight north until I call to turn to the west. There's a line at three fathoms here that'll take us to a passage to the harbor." I went forward after checking the course, repeating Rhames instructions for finding the channel in my head and dropped the lead line over the side. We were just shy of three fathoms now, and I knew we had a few feet below the keel. A few minutes later the lead line indicated we had reached our spot and I called for Rory to turn. I had to admit the girl was good with a boat. Instead of making a hard turn she called back my order and waited for Swift and Syd to adjust the sails. She then turned in a wide arc. The fore and aft mains and topsails were full and I watched as the men moved to the bowsprit and unfurled the jibs.

I coiled the lead line and went back to the helm. I needed the speed of the boat to calculate the time to reach the passage and held the knot line, splitting the coil between my hands. I waited until the men had the jibs rigged and the wind filled the canvas before dropping it. I counted to thirty before retrieving the line and counting the knots. The boat was making close to nine knots. I left Rory with directions to hold course and went below to plot our position on the chart.

A pair of dividers was in the drawer and I used the latitude lines to estimate the mileage and time to reach the channel. Sixty-four miles separated us from our destination and I divided that by our speed. If the wind held, we would reach the passage in seven hours. It would be too late to navigate the narrow channel in low light, so I planned on anchoring for the night just outside of it. I relaxed slightly. We were fortunate that the boat we had stumbled on had a shallow draft. At eight feet below the waterline, we could skirt the shallows where the larger vessels, including the Navy, were restricted to the deeper water.

I went back on deck after double checking my calculations and saw Rory at the helm, a smile on her face which she tried to hide with a snarl as I approached. "We should reach the passage to the harbor around sunset. We'll have to anchor for the night before making our approach. It's too narrow to try it in low light."

"Don't think I'll change my mind in another night," she said.

I came close to walking away but turned to her instead, "Might not be as easy as I thought when we make port. These men were smugglers." I watched as she turned to me.

"There're barrels of spices and bales of tobacco below as well as some unmarked crates, bound for New Orleans from the log. I suspect they were slavers as well from the chains in the hold."

"That's not going to change my opinion one bit. Pirates, smugglers, the lot of you are the same. If a pirate steals from a smuggler, does that make him less of a pirate?"

I was growing tired of fighting with her and left her at the wheel. Swift and Syd were leaning against the foremast, talking quietly, but stopped as I approached. I gave them our position and my plan to anchor outside of the channel tonight. They nodded, and continued their conversation as I moved forward to the bowsprit to think. Rory was content by herself at the helm and I was clearly not welcome in the other men's conversation.

I sat on the narrow point of the bowsprit, both legs extended toward the water, catching spray on my bare feet as the bow sliced through the small waves and thought about what we needed. First was to get Rory off the boat. Her presence was unsettling to not only me, but from the way the other men avoided her, I could tell they would welcome her departure as well. Next we needed supplies and news. Learning the location of the Naval fleet, who they had captured and which pirates were still at large in these waters was essential before we began to make a plan for the future. I had brought enough coin to buy supplies and a long boat that could be towed from our craft. From the looks of the narrow passage on the chart, it was water that I only intended to try once. With a long boat we could move east on the ocean side from the harbor, anchor off one of the islands in deeper water and row through the shallow water to Rhames and the others.

I must have fallen asleep because the sun was well past its zenith when a large wave splashed me. The wind had picked up, and we were clearly moving faster than I had estimated earlier. I shook the sleep from my head and walked to the helm where I checked our course and dropped the knot line.

"How long has the wind been up?" I asked Rory, who was still at the wheel.

"Just now," she said.

I retrieved and counted ten knots now, estimated the time from the sun and went below to calculate our position and change my estimated time of our arrival. From the position I had plotted earlier, I changed the calculation to our current speed and figured our arrival an hour earlier. With the chart back in its case, I went back on deck and looked at the chain of islands in the distance, watching for the gap that would mark the channel.

As if on cue, an hour later I saw it and called to Swift and Syd to drop sail and ready the anchor. I yelled back to Rory to steer south, toward shallower water and went forward to drop the lead. Fifteen minutes later it showed us in two fathoms and I signaled for the anchor to be dropped.

Chapter Ten

A short but strong storm blew in overnight bringing gusty winds and rain. I was up at the first drops and stayed on deck, hunkered under a tarp to keep watch through the night. The wind had shifted to the north and we swung on the anchor as it changed. My primary focus was on our position, for if the anchor pulled with the wind from this quarter we would ground. I was wet and cold by the time the sun rose, but the storm had played out. I wasted no time in ordering the anchor raised and the fore and main sails set. The tailwind allowed us to cruise on a dead run with a following sea. Not the fastest point of sail, but to navigate the narrow channel there was no better condition. The boat moved forward as the booms were pushed out perpendicular to the boat and the sails filled.

I chose to put Rory back on the wheel, which allowed me to work the rigging and drop the lead every few minutes. Syd and Swift tuned the sails and the boat shot forward. My biggest concern was the depth of the water under the keel. So long as we stayed in the channel we would arrive in the harbor. I kept a careful eye on the chain of islands to the left, careful to run parallel to them as Rhames had described.

The sun came out and I could see the shoals to either side of the boat. The water was so easy to read from my vantage point midway up the rigging on the main mast that I abandoned the lead and called directions to Rory. An hour later the big island came into view, the tips of several masts visible over the flat land. I ordered the foresail shortened and then dropped as the mainsail was providing enough propulsion to enter the harbor safely. We turned around the point protecting the entrance, narrowly missing a sandbar, dropped the mainsail into the lazy jacks, and coasted to a stop by several other boats of similar design. I called ahead to Syd to drop anchor and the boat swung into the wind as the hook caught.

I looked over toward the pier where several small launches and one larger ship were tied off and wondered what lay ahead on the streets that spilled from the harbor. In the four years I had spent with the crew, I had never been allowed into a city and as I thought back, the last visit to anything larger than a shanty town was our departure from London five years ago. I eagerly anticipated the foreign sights and sounds and could barely wait to get ashore when my excitement faded as Rory came toward me and I realized we had no launch. As I kicked myself for not keeping at least one of the canoes I saw a small boat being rowed toward us.

She stood by my side as a boat approached with a well-dressed man sitting in the bow, rowed by a dark-skinned man behind him. I assumed he was the harbormaster and reached into my pocket fingering the coins.

The man put his hands to his mouth, "Ahoy."

"Ahoy, sir. We would like to anchor overnight and hire a launch to the pier."

"Aye, wouldn't we all. It'll cost you some coin, boy. Send your master to negotiate."

The insult stung, but I kept my composure. "My age has nothing to do with it. I am master of this vessel."

"Well then, if you've coin, I'll accept it. Climb down and we'll take you to shore."

I looked back at the crew who nodded. I started to descend and as I reached the last rung on the rope ladder, I looked up and saw Rory following.

"Don't be looking up my skirt. And don't be thinking I'll trust you to go alone." She hurried down the ladder and reached the boat before I or the men aboard could react. We sat and watched the harbor in silence as we were rowed to shore.

Without a word the black man spun the boat with a hard back-paddle and pulled toward the pier. We reached the wooden structure and climbed onto the dock. The well-dressed man led us to a small building located where the pier met solid land and we entered what I expected was his office. I couldn't help but notice a brand new American flag hanging on the wall. *Curious*, I thought, *the last I had heard the island was in Spanish hands.*

The room was cluttered and dim, with light filtering in through shuttered windows. I expected it would be hot in the summer, but this time of year it was comfortable. His desk was cluttered with papers and log books and a small monkey clucked and strained against its chain in the corner. He motioned us to the two chairs in front of his desk and cleared a small space where he placed his beefy hands.

"Are we in America now?" I asked.

"Just last month the bloody Spanish pulled out and my boss, fellow named Simonton bought this rock and probably overpaid at two thousand dollars. Now, state your business and cargo. I'll need to know the crew as well," he said as he struck a match and lit a pipe.

"The lady here is in need of a vessel to take her back to England. Otherwise we are three men including myself aboard. We are in need of provisions and we'll be on our way."

His eyes widened and he smiled at the mention of Rory, "I can maybe help with the lady. Nothing leaves directly from here, but there's a merchant ship bound for St. Augustine. From there one could find passage." He looked back at me with a stern face. "A bit of gold will buy your stay."

I was unsure what a bit of gold referred to, but not wanting to reveal my naivety, reached into my pocket, took out a single gold coin and nonchalantly tossed it on the desk.

"It'll take two more of those, boy."

I knew he was testing me. "I'll add a shilling for your time, but no more." I reached in my pocket and carefully picked out one of the silver coins, hoping he could not see the gold.

"You drive a hard bargain, but as long as you're not wastin' my time, I'll take it." He grabbed the two coins off the desk. "If you have a list, I'll take care of it for you."

I assumed it was another ploy to separate me from whatever money I had left and shook my head. "I'd prefer to look around for myself."

He nodded. "As for the lady. Who will be paying her passage?"

I needed his help here. "You help negotiate a fair price and I'll pay you a guinea for your time."

"Now you're thinking, son," he looked at Rory and smiled again revealing a mouth full of yellow and rotten teeth. "Your timing couldn't be better. That ship at the dock is scheduled to leave in a few hours on the outgoing tide." He rose and went out the door.

I stumbled behind him thinking this was moving too fast. We walked past several open dories unloading turtles onto the docks where workers loaded the huge shelled amphibians into wheelbarrows and carted them away. As we approached the larger ship I noticed it was rigged as ours, but was at least one hundred feet in length and had a beam almost twice ours. Derricks mounted on the pier with a block and tackle hanging from a boom were loading turtles and bales into the hold. A man of mixed blood stood watching, a cigar stuck in his mouth. He sensed our presence and turned after a long pause while a crate was loaded.

"And what have we here?"

I started to speak, but the harbormaster cut me off. "Girl'll need passage. Can you accommodate her?"

"I suspect she'll be needing a cabin," he squinted at her.

"I don't need anything fancy, just a bit of privacy," she said.

"A bit of privacy, is it?" He turned to me, "And you?"

"I'm a cousin just arranging for her passage. What kind of fare are you asking?"

He rubbed the stubble on his chin and blew a large puff of smoke toward the water. "Be a dozen pounds, and that'll feed her as well."

It was more than I anticipated, but with a fortune in treasure back at the island and his the only boat leaving, I felt no need to negotiate. I looked at Rory and she nodded. "We have a deal then." I reached into my pocket and removed the coins, but was unable to hide the remaining gold from the harbormaster. I handed him the coins and he took her shoulder as if she were chattel. She instinctively fought back and he kept his grasp, a smile crossing his face again.

"Just follow me, luv, and I'll show you to your cabin."

Without a glimpse backwards she walked the gangway set between the dock and the boat. I stood on tiptoes anxious for a last look at her, but the captain caught my eye and leered back. As I turned to the harbormaster I heard what I thought was a woman scream. But the captain ordered the crew to pull the plank and let lose the lines before I could react. Within seconds, as I stood there dumfounded, poles emerged from the deck and pushed the boat into the harbor. Several other men were in the rigging and raised the sails. My jaw dropped again as I heard her, but the wind had her sails and the boat moved away.

Chapter Eleven

"So, about those provisions," the man asked.

I ignored him as I stared after the boat, listening as I thought I heard her scream again. He asked again and I turned to him, his rotten teeth showing in a vague smile. "Never mind," I said and walked to an open fishing boat pulling to the dock.

The man standing in the bow cocked his head at me and I acknowledged that I would receive the line he was about to toss. As I grabbed it, I noticed the harbormaster looking out to sea as if expecting something.

"I can get some good deals for you. Maybe a meal and a woman."

He had seen my gold and I knew his aim. I followed his gaze to the harbor entrance and saw a frigate on the horizon. It was still a ways away and with the sun setting behind it I couldn't see any detail, but it looked familiar.

I still held the line in my hand and ignored the fisherman calling to me. I turned to the harbormaster, "You know that ship?"

The fisherman yelled to me as his boat slammed against a pile. I tied off the bow and went to the stern to help with the other line. I looked back at the harbormaster who was still watching the frigate as it closed on us, a large smile on his face. The man had seen my gold, and might have suspected our profession. Another look at the boat and I knew where I had seen it before. I could not be positive from this distance, but it appeared to be the Navy ship that had sunk the Floridablanca.

"I'll take your gold and say nothing to them," the harbormaster said.

He confirmed my suspicion. Without a word, I tossed the stern line, still in my hand back to the boat, ran to the bow and untied the line. With it in my hand, I jumped into the boat. The three men stared at me until I reached into my pocket and withdrew a handful of coins.

"A ride to the ship and your cargo," I said as I extended my hand with the coins.

The older man grabbed them and ordered the two crewmen to their oars. In seconds, the boat had turned and was moving fast toward our ship. I leaned back toward the older man and pointed to a route that would take us out of sight of the Navy boat.

We reached the schooner a few tense minutes later and I yelled to the men, who were leaning over the starboard rail staring at the frigate as it approached. They ran across the deck and tossed the rope ladder down to me. I grabbed for the rungs and yelled orders as I climbed. After jumping the rail, I joined to help them load the cargo. We threw lines and loaded the water casks, reluctantly leaving the turtle and fish behind. I hadn't wanted to waste the time, but we would at least need the water if we had to stay at sea or hide among the small Keys to avoid the frigate and we had offloaded our stores at the island thinking we could provision here. Before the last keg hit the deck, the fishing boat was moving away, the grunts of the men working the oars audible as they strained to put distance between us.

I looked to the frigate which had anchored and was dropping

longboats to the water. "Slowly now, bring us tight on the anchor and ready the sails," I called to the men and continued to watch the frigate as it prepared to drop the boats and secure the ship. I could feel us moving now as Syd and Swift had the chain around the winch and pulled us close to perpendicular above the anchor, tie the line off and start to ready the sails. In this position the anchor would pull at our first movement.

I was about to call for it to be raised when I realized that a little patience would work to our advantage. We had the element of surprise. They may have suspected us as pirates, but with the frigate anchored in the entrance to the harbor and the long boats in the water they were confident all the boats were trapped. The men looked at me for direction, the looks on their faces clearly distressed.

"Easy. As soon as their men are in the longboats and the rest of the crew is in the rigging stowing the sails, we make our move."

They acknowledged my subterfuge. We would have to pass the frigate and within cannon range, to make our escape, but with a good part of their crew in the rigging stowing and lashing the sails for the night, and the men in the longboats too slow to give us chase, I expected we could sail right by with minimal damage. The time was right as the longboats were loaded and ready to move. At least a dozen figures were visible in the rigging of the ship.

"Raise the sails," I called as I ran to the anchor. I had thought we might have time to pull it, but a glance at the longboats moving toward us forced my hand. It would be costly to lose, but might save our lives. I reached for a sea ax mounted to the foremast, raised the ax over my head and slammed the chain just as the sails filled. The link held, and I wound up again. Syd and Swift were still working the sails and the boat was straining against the weight of the anchor and chain. I closed my eyes and brought the ax high overhead. As hard as I could I brought the iron blade down onto the chain and cringed as it hit, the shock of metal hitting metal reverberating through my body. I glanced down in dismay as the ax head lay in two pieces, but the chain had split, and I ran to the helm as it rattled overboard.

"Full sail," I called to the men as I corrected our course. It was dangerous to have that much canvas out in these close quarters, but we needed all the speed the boat could muster. The sails snapped as they filled and the boat lurched forward. The men were out of the rigging standing by me and we exchanged a quick grin as we picked up speed. "Best set the jibs as well," I ordered as I set course to run by the frigate.

We were less than a quarter mile away when I heard the whistle blow aboard the Navy boat. The men scrambled out of the rigging and the remaining crew moved to the guns. I needed five minutes to get past them and out of range of their cannon and knew it would be close. Suddenly I heard a shot off our stern and looked back at the longboats as they fired their small guns at us. The projectiles fell well short and I refocused on the frigate.

Time seemed to stand still as we moved slowly by the frigate. We were close enough to hear every order and I clenched my jaw, waiting for the call to fire. With a burst, we gained a little speed as the jibs caught the breeze one at a time and we were by them just as a whistle blew and the cannon fired. I didn't want to look behind at our demise, but couldn't resist. There was nothing to be done, as we were moving away at our maximum speed with every inch of sail raised. I heard water splash and saw several balls hit the water, not ten feet from us. I breathed in relief as we pulled away.

Syd and Swift were back at the helm and we let out a loud whoop as we realized we had escaped. Minutes later, we rounded the point and found open water, the only thing visible of the frigate was the top of its masts over the flat land. We moved faster through the water now that we had left the protection of the harbor and I realized, that at least for now we were safe. It would take too much time for the frigate to regain its longboats, raise anchor and set sail. I expected they would pursue, but it would take them too much time because of the speed or our craft. I studied the chain of islands just coming into sight as we rounded the last bit of land, each gap between them allowed an opportunity for us to to hide.

TIDES OF FORTUNE
episode four
CAYO
HUESO
STEVEN BECKER

Chapter One

ISyd and Swift were not in sight and I ran to the companionway, stuck my head in, and yelled for them. "Bring a torch and hurry down to the hold." I waited until I heard movement and went forward to the hatch just aft of the bowsprit. It was stuck, nailed shut to prevent the prisoners from escaping. I grabbed the ax that was lashed to the mast and tried to use the broken blade to pry it open. The wood splintered, but I ignored the damage and stuck the edge of the blade between the deck boards and the cover. Finally, the hatch gave way and the stench almost knocked me off my feet as air flowed through the hold.

"What's this all about?" Swift asked as he held the lantern over the opening.

"There's men in there. Bastards weren't just smugglers - they're slavers as well." I took the lantern and descended the ladder two steps at a time. "Bring the ax," I called up as my feet hit the deck.

The three of us crossed through the main hold together and peered into the forward compartment. The added ventilation provided by the hatch, had sucked some of the smell from the room, but I still had to put my shirt tail to my nose to breath. Swift and Syd followed my lead as we went in and held the light. Half a dozen bodies were shackled to the boat, three on each side of the hold.

"Hold on, I have an idea," I said as I climbed back to the deck. I went to the captains quarters, pulled out the drawer below the desk and started rummaging through its contents. Toward the back I found what I was looking for and withdrew a ring of keys. I went back down to the hold and found Swift and Syd leaning outside the door.

"Can't take the smell for long," one of them muttered.

I ignored them and went through the door to the first man. Swift held the light for me as I started to try each key in the locks. On the third try, I found it and released the man. "Carry him out, I called to Syd who was still standing by the door. I didn't wait for a reply but went to the next man and freed him.

A few minutes later we had them in the main hold and I went to check each one. Two still clung to life, but the other four had passed. One was unconscious and I made him comfortable before returning to the first man. His eyes were open, but when I held the light to them, they were vacant. "Get some water," I called and tried to figure out what to do, wishing Lucy was here.

Syd went on deck and lowered a bucket into the hold. I took the ladle from it and put it to the man's parched lips. Some primal urge must have come from deep within him as he shot to life and grabbed the ladle from my hands. He put it to his face, wasting most of the water down his shirt. I took it back and refilled it for him. This time he managed to drink.

"We can leave these two down here for the time being, but we've got to get the dead off the boat." Syd and Swift nodded in agreement and went to fetch the line attached to the block and tackle. The bodies released gas and fluid as we lifted them and we stood in a pool of noxious fluids as we worked, some of them probably ours as I heard one of the men vomit. Finally, the work was done and we sat in the fresh air on deck.

"Bloody bit of luck," Swift said. "Something about you always finding people to save."

I knew he was referring to our rescue of Rory and then the adoption of Blue and Lucy, who were now hiding out on an island with Rhames, and the treasure. I ignored his comment, went to the casks and lowered another pail of water down before following it to see about the two men still alive.

"Can you talk?" I asked the man who sat upright.

He looked around vacantly and rolled over onto his side. I did the best I could to make him comfortable and went back on deck.

"The one's asleep and the other's still out." I leaned over the rail wondering what to do. The water swirled and something large jumped near the ship. It was dark, the moon still below the horizon, but I knew the sharks had found the dead men.

Chapter Two

My watch started at midnight and after observing our position I went below to check on the two men. I had lain on my bunk tossing and turning, but sleep had eluded me. Light from the waxing gibbous moon, a sliver from full, flooded the hold and I could see the faces of the men without the need for a lantern. They were both asleep, Swift said the one man who had gained consciousness had eaten some food and drank when I relieved him of his watch. I went to check that the other man was still alive and could see his chest rise and fall as he breathed.

He shifted and I thought he was awake until I realized that it was the boat moving on the sandbar below, the keel struggling to release itself from the suction of the sand. I returned to the forward hold to continue my search for a spare anchor. The light was dim as I moved forward, and I thought about going above for a lantern but the boat shifted again. The sound of the water racing against the hull as the tide rose increased my urgency as I dug through the sails.

The boat shifted again, and I knew we only had minutes before we would be free of the sand bar and at the mercy of the tide. There was nothing in the hold, but in the dim light I could see another hatch in the floor. I went to it with some trepidation after what the last hatch I had opened revealed, held my breath, pulled the latch, and opened the wooden cover. The sound of water sloshing around told me it was the bilge and I was just about to shut the cover and look elsewhere when a thought struck me.

I jumped down into the ankle deep water and waited for my eyes to adjust to the dark. The sound of the sea was louder here as I started to feel around for the ballast. I bumped into a board stuck from the floor and not knowing what it was moved around it. The boat shifted again and I stumbled, unable to gain footing on the uneven floor. On my knees I ran my hands along the objects, and found a mixture of materials. With no time to look further I grabbed a smooth rectangular shaped piece of metal and tried to pull it off the floor. It resisted my efforts and I scurried back to the main hold seeking the rope attached to the boom.

The boat moved again, this time turning with the tide. "Help!" I called down the companionway to wake the sleeping men. With no time to wait I yelled again and went toward the stern. I grabbed the rope hanging from the block and tackle, pulled the slack with me as I climbed back into the hold, made my way back to the bilge and started to work the rope around the heavy object. Satisfied, I went back to the main hold and saw Swift and Syd standing above me.

"Pull the line," I called and raced back for the ballast. I could feel the rope come under tension as I reached the object and started to guide it through the ship. I hoped it had not damaged anything as it banged against the bulkheads around the lower hatch. Through the sail locker and then into the main hold I guided the weight until it sat below the main hatch.

"What the bloody …" Swift started.

I ignored him and climbed the ladder. "Anchor. Its all we've got. Hurry up and lets get it over the side." Together we hauled on the line and the weight rose through the opening. I let the other men take the weight and went to the boom to swing it outboard. With a final grunt, the men hoisted the object over the side.

"Let her go and tie off the line." I called out as it crashed into the water. Line whipped through our hands as the heavy weight sought the bottom. Syd grabbed the bitter end and tied it to a metal cleat near the transom and we waited. The boat seemed to lift and turn beneath us as the tide lifted the keel from the sand.

We waited to see if the weight would hold, unable to do anything but watch, as the tide swung the boat. Feeling a tug, we exchanged a smile as the line came taut and the boat settled. Before we could congratulate ourselves we looked in shock as a man emerged from the hold. Syd and I went to him, but he shrugged us off and gained the deck under his own power.

"Mason," he said with a heavy accent and extended his hand.

We exchanged names and stood there staring at each other.

"I'm guessing y'all are not the men that took the ship."

I hesitated not knowing if he was referring to us or the smugglers. "We ran across the ship up the coast."

"So, you pirated a pirate ship," he asked.

Apparently he hadn't sustained a head wound as he cut to the quick of our situation. "Something like that. But slavers we are not. You and your friend are free men now."

"What about the rest?" he asked.

"Sorry," I answered. Together we went to the galley.

We had several hours to wait until the sun was up and it would be safe to navigate. I brought him some food and water which he ate and drank greedily. I left him after a time and went to adjust the boat to her new anchorage. Satisfied the anchor held the boat in deep enough water and in the center of the channel, I went below and we told our stories while we waited for daylight.

They had been a crew of a dozen, running fish, turtles and tobacco from Havana to New Orleans in an older wide beamed ketch when a storm had brought them into Key West. They had left the port after the weather cleared and noticed a boat shadowing them as they moved up the coast. They were apprehended and boarded several hours later with half their crew dying in the fight. The pirates took the cargo and scuttled their boat, forcing the remaining men to the hold, where they hadn't seen daylight in what he guessed was a week.

"Four were dead, and there's another below. He's alive," I finished our story leaving out the murders of the pirates.

"What are your intentions then?" he asked just as the first ray of light showed above the line of water to the east.

My plan at the moment was to find a deep water pass to the Gulf side and our island, but without an accurate chart or guide, that would prove impossible.

"Time to get underway, we need to move." I said as I rose from the bench. We went to the deck and I took the helm while Syd and Swift went into the rigging. Without a command, they unfurled the mainsail and the light breeze moved the boat forward on the rope holding the ballast. They climbed down and went to the bow. Swift took in the slack, wound it around the winch and with Syd's help hauled the weight toward the boat.

There was no way to secure the object and as it came aboard so we dropped it into the hold. I couldn't help but notice the sheen to it, but had to wait until we were clear of the shoals before examining it. The boat was floating free and with a light touch I was able to steer toward deeper water. Once I felt we were safely in Hawk's channel, the band of deep water running between land and the reef, I turned the helm over to Syd and went to inspect the object.

Mason followed me into the hold and I brushed my hand against the metal using my shirt to clean the scum from its surface. It shone back, a silver hue.

Chapter Three

I set the mystery of the ballast from my mind as the need to navigate through the narrow channel became paramount. The sun was high enough to show the shallows a light green and I called out directions from the rigging. The breeze was light from the northeast, causing us to trim the sails as we beat into it. The channel was wide, but I dared not press the edges as the huge hunks of coral that formed the reef would tear the bottom from our boat. The area I judged to be safe was too narrow to tack which caused us to creep forward into the wind, with the sails luffing instead of full.

I climbed down from my perch after we were clear of the last obstacle and ordered a course to the east. There was some room to maneuver in the channel between land and the reef, but if we were to make any progress today we would have to cross the reef line into deeper water. I went to the helm and glanced around the deck for Mason, but he was nowhere in sight. Syd was a the wheel and must have caught my look.

"Went into the hold to tend his mate," he said as I approached.

"Bad deal those men went through."

"Aye," he replied.

"We need to cross the reef and head for deeper water if we are to make any distance today."

"That's serious business."

I looked out to sea and knew his concern. Since the beginning of Spanish conquest, hundreds of years ago, ships had followed this stretch of water between the islands to our left and the Bahamas somewhere over the horizon to our right. It was common knowledge that the reef had claimed more ships than pirates had. "All the same. If the Navy is giving chase we need to stay ahead of them."

He cut the wheel to starboard and the sails snapped as the wind filled them. I could see the veins in his arms as he fought the wheel against the weather helm. "Back her a few degrees and she'll ride better."

Syd moved the wheel back to port.

"What's all this?" Swift called as he came on deck. "Can't a man get some sleep?"

"Course is set now, but you might stay a bit. We are going to cross the reef in a few minutes," I said.

"Bloody hell. That reef's more dangerous than a bent tooth whore."

I ignored the comment and climbed the rigging, grasping to the handholds as the boat rocked back and forth fighting against the seas. Thankfully the sun would be near its zenith when we crossed the reef, revealing the detail of the dangers below our keel. Ahead I could see the light green water of the shallows, with some brown spots mixed in. It was difficult to tell the depth of the shallows, but it was the brown spots that we had to avoid at all costs as these were the coral heads that rose from the bottom, often only inches below the surface.

A dark channel caught my eye and I directed Syd toward it. Swift called out the depth below us as we crossed the barrier and I climbed down relieved, when the call reached six fathoms. With thirty odd feet below us I knew we were safe, at least until we had to cross back to anchor for the night.

Back on deck, I gave the course to Syd and went to the log line to determine our speed. It came back with a few feet over seven and I went down to my cabin to chart our position and find an anchorage for the night. With my dagger I sharpened the thin piece of lead and went to work on the chart. Tacking was the hardest maneuver to chart as the ship was not moving from point to point, but rather sailing a zig zag line to utilize the wind. The best point of sail was forty five degrees off our stern, either way and I went to work using the compass rose and the parallel rules to draw faint lines on the chart. The task was further complicated by the vessel's lack of a chronometer. I had left orders to remain on course for an hour, an easy unit to measure as it was about four fingers held to the sky in the path of the sun, but the higher the sun was in the sky, the less accurate it became. I expected to feel the boats course change shortly and as if on cue, Syd turned ninety degrees and the sails shifted to the other side of the boat.

I used the dividers set to seven and a half miles, or an hours progress, then traced a line forty five degrees to the wind the length of the dividers. Back and forth I drew each line ninety degrees to the last until the fifth inshore line ended close to a large island, marked Indian Key. I checked the area of the reef the line passed through and although there was little detail, there were no hazards marked. If all went to plan, Indian Key would be our anchorage for the night.

I went back on deck and gave the course and changes to Swift who had taken the wheel.

"Have you seen the man?"

"He's a strange one, talks like he has marbles in his mouth. Been up and down from the hold a half dozen times. Reckon he's down there now."

I left the helm and went to the hold. "Can I bring you anything before I come down?" I called into the void.

"A bit of food would be welcome," Mason said.

With a hunk of turtle meat in my hand, I descended into the hold. The air was stagnant and had the reek of death on it. The ventilation provided by the forward deck hatch was lost as we had closed it before we left the anchorage. One large wave over the bow with the hatch open would have flooded the hold. I breathed through my mouth, hoping I would get used to it. "How is he?"

"Could be worse," Mason said. "Came to a few hours ago. Hasn't said much, but he's been drinking water and asked for food."

I handed him the meat. "We're glad for it. That lot we put off the boat deserved what they got. Can we get him on deck? The air's a lot better there."

"Let him rest a bit. Maybe in an hour or so," Mason said as he pushed a torn piece of meat toward the mans mouth. He made a sniffing face like a rabbit and took the offered food.

"So, do you care to tell me about the silver in the bilge?"

"Reckon since you know already there ain't no harm," he pulled another piece of meat and fed the man. "We were working as divers using these new helmets that attach to tubes leading to the surface where the men use bellows to pump air. Not real comfortable, but to be underwater and breath is a different view of the world.

"Undersea helmets," I repeated, my attention riveted on him. "Divers." I felt the tension of command fall from me as he explained about working underwater.

"You see, we would seek out wrecked boats in shallow water and use the helmets to salvage them. Pulled all sorts of treasure and such from the clutches of the sandy bottom. Problem was the pirates knew what we were doing and would wait until we finished before swooping in and taking our rewards. Captain got tired of it and stashed the silver bars in the bilge, but the pirates found them and killed him."

"I thought you said you were traders?"

"Wasn't the need to tell you before you found the silver."

"Why didn't he seek protection?" I asked forgiving the lie and fascinated by his story.

"That was kind of the way it worked. The pirates would leave us some trinkets for supplies and never threatened harm to us or the boat. They just wanted what they said was their due for protecting us. Personally, I didn't see much of the protection."

I sat back, the smell and still air no longer affecting me, and watched him feed the other man. There was something here in what the man said that would solve our problem of trading or selling the pirate loot. "Supposing we helped you in this salvage business. Make you and your mate full partners in anything we find."

He looked up at me. "I figured you lot for pirates."

"Times are changing. If you can forgive us our past, I think we could have a future together."

"Let me see how my friend here gets on. Seeing as we have nothing else on the horizon, we might could work something out. But, I'll tell you now, pirating is out of the question. We aim to earn our fortune, but the only victim is the sea."

This sounded too good to be true and I couldn't help but smile thinking of the possibilities of legal pirating. I think there was even a name for it.

"Ship!" I heard a cry from the deck and climbed the ladder to see what was on the horizon.

Chapter Four

It was the frigate, beating into the wind in the channel between the reef and land. The captain had made the choice to fight the wind, rather than tack as we had. What he lost in speed, he gained in the ability to chase his prey. By staying close to shore he would be able to see the masts of any ship trying to hide amongst the islands. We were on a port tack heading toward the reef and I had little time to calculate our position. I ran to my cabin and pulled the chart from its cover. With no time to drop a lead or knot line, I had to estimate.

I put a pin where I expected we were and went above to look at the position of the frigate. The captain would have the same charts as we did and would be cautious to cross the reef line. We had to lose them now as we didn't have the luxury, as he did, to play it safe and shadow us until night fell. The choice between facing the reef in the dark or the Navy ship was one I didn't want to make. To make matters more complicated, if I chose to stay out to sea and avoid the reef, we took the chance of crossing into the gulfstream which would carry us too far north.

The best option was to cross the reef behind the frigate. They would be unwilling or unable to come about in the tight channel and we would have the advantage of a favorable tack. The frigate drew at least two fathoms from the looks of her and would not be able to follow us into the shallows. If we could make Indian Key, the Navy would be reluctant to send their boats into the reportedly hostile port.

I went back on deck, a spyglass in one hand and the chart in the other, careful to shield the delicate paper from the elements with my shirt. Using the protection provided by the companionway I removed it and tried to orient myself with the land to the left. If I could approximate our position, I could try and plot a path through the reef.

The island chain spread out in front of us, each Key a different shape and size, making them hard to place on the chart. With the spyglass to my eye, I could see more detail, but the motion of the waves would not allow me to concentrate long enough to place them. I thought I saw the tips of several masts in the distance and took a chance that the island I hoped to be Indian Key lay ahead. A glance back confirmed the frigate was still in the channel. We would have to tack again to come in behind it.

I returned the chart and glass to the cabin and went back on deck. Mason was with Swift at the wheel and Syd was in the bowsprit working the lead as we approached the reef.

"There's where we're going," I pointed. "But we need to tack again, then reverse course before turning behind the frigate."

"What of the reef?" Swift asked.

"We've no choice," I said and called to Syd for the depth. We needed to get close to the reef before turning to give the illusion that we were going through it. If we appeared to remain on our course, the captain of the frigate would assume we would continue the tack in front of them and continue the pursuit. Syd called back that we were in ten fathoms and dropping. I looked forward and saw the dangerous green water ahead. "Keep calling," I yelled into the wind and turned to Swift. "When we hit six fathoms make your turn."

I could only stand and watch now as Syd called out the depth and Swift clung to the wheel.

"What can I do?" Mason asked.

"I'd go below and make sure your mate's secure," I said without taking my eyes off the frigate. The captain had fallen for our ruse and continued his course and speed, waiting for us to cross the reef line in front of them. I could see figures in the rigging watching us and more on deck preparing the guns. We were in green water now and I waited for the turn. Finally Syd called six fathoms and Swift spun the wheel. The boat turned and the sails snapped into their new position. We were running southwest now and away from the frigate. I checked the sun and saw we had another hour or so before dark.

"They think we're running," Swift said.

"Right. Let'em think we're heading for the Bahamas." Fearing a run-in with the British, I calculated the captain of the frigate wouldn't cross the stream to follow us into the small island chain. "We keep this tack for half an hour and then cut behind them in the fading light. Then it's just a matter of getting past the reef then."

"You mean to run the reef in the dark," Mason asked as he climbed back on deck.

"A bit before," I said with a little swagger in my voice, that was not shared by my gut.

"It's going to take more than one lead to get through. If you've got another, I can help. Your man can work his line and I'll toss one ahead and let it drag the bottom." Mason said.

I nodded and went to my cabin to see if there was a spare. He was right. With two lines we would get a better picture of the danger below us as we tried to navigate through the maze of corals and shallows. I found a line and went back on deck. "Here," I handed it to him and watched him go forward.

"He might be some use after all," Swift said. "How long 'til the turn?"

I was distracted as a wave of flying fish left the water in front of the boat and took it for a sign. The frigate was in front of us now, a dot on the horizon outlined in the setting sun. In this light we would be almost invisible to them. "Make the turn now."

He cut the wheel and the boat turned back toward land, its angle would clearly bring it behind the frigate. "Right then," I called to Mason and Syd. "Start calling when we reach ten fathoms." I went to the foremast and began to climb the rigging for a better vantage, but the glare of the sun on the water made the color changes indistinguishable. It might as well have been dark for all I could see. I climbed back down and went to Swift. We stared at the dark water in front of us waiting for the men in the bow to call out the ten fathom line.

With nothing to do but wait, I started to think ahead to our anchorage and beyond. We needed to get back to the island and reunite the crew. Swift and Syd knew nothing of the silver in the bilge, and were anxious about the treasure we left on the island. Upon reaching Indian Key I hoped to buy a longboat with the coin left in my pocket, leave a watch on the boat and use it to navigate the shallow waters to the island.

"Six fathoms," Syd called out. He had just retrieved his line, measured it with the span of his arms and quickly tossed it ahead of the boat.

"Aye, six under the keel," Mason called to confirm.

We were moving too fast and I yelled to Syd to help me reef the sails. His lead probing under the boat was not much use now.

"Five and dropping, " Mason yelled.

Syd and I struggled with the fore topsail, finally dropping it. We climbed down and released the halyard for the fore mainsail, then repeated the process on the main topsail. The boat slowed and I had a moment of doubt that I had removed too much canvas and we would lose headway, making it impossible to steer.

"Three and a half," Mason called.

We were in twenty feet now and it would be only moments before we knew if the reef was safe to pass here. I climbed halfway into the rigging to see if the coral was breaking the surface or if the wave action was changed by an unseen object just below.

"Two fathoms and holding," Mason called.

This was the point of no return. We had only four feet below our keel. If the depth held, we would be through the deadly reef. I jumped onto the deck and ran toward the bowsprit unable to wait for our fate.

Mason worked the lead on the bottom. I held my breath as he retrieved a few feet of line, indicating the water was getting shallower.

"A bit over two." He gradually released some line. "Three now."

I could only wait.

"Four fathoms," he called.

I knew we had made it, and we exchanged grins. My eyes strained as I looked ahead and I could barely make out the dot on the horizon that was the frigate. It would be well ahead of us when we crossed its path, and I turned toward land looking for a suitable anchorage.

Chapter Five

The reef was notorious for the wrecks it had claimed and I considered us to be fortunate to not be counted among their numbers. But, for all our luck in evading the frigate, we were off our mark. Ahead was a long island, with a small landmass in front, which I had guessed to be Indian Key, but Mason had told me otherwise.

"You've got the landmarks right, but the scale is wrong," he said as we sat over the chart table in my cabin. "See here," he pointed to Indian Key and ran his fingers over the longer Matacumbe Key below it. "This is where we are," he moved his finger to Duck Key with the longer Vaca Key behind it. "If you don't know these waters, they likely look the same from a distance. Closer in, I reckon you would have figured it out."

"But we are west of Indian Key by twenty odd miles."

"There's some currents in these waters that'll fool you. There was no time to run the log line yesterday and with the wind from the northeast as it is, the water'll be movin' in that direction as well. Could be close to a three knot current."

I traced the route back to the area where we had crossed the reef, close to a hazard marked as Sombrero Key. "We passed by that? And you knew?"

"Don't reckon there was a choice, was there?"

He was right and I realized just how close we had come to destruction. "You know this area then?"

"Been through once or twice. You're one of the lucky ones to make it past Sombrero in one piece. Some gold and silver's sitting out there for the taking."

Impressed by his knowledge I did the calculation in my head and realized a three knot current running against us would put us just where he said we were. "Is there a good anchorage here?"

He pointed to the western tip of the long island. "There's a small village in a deep harbor there called Port Monroe. More like a couple of shacks than a village and the island protecting the anchorage is big enough the Navy ship won't be able to see our masts behind it."

The spot looked suitable and I was happy that he had no objections to our dodging the Navy ship. Possibly the fortune in silver in the bilge had something to do with that, but I took him at face value.

"I need to tend my friend," he got up to leave.

"How is he?" I asked. "If we can get back to these islands," I pointed to the chart, "I have a woman that is a healer there."

"He'll be needin' something. Right now he's alive, but a fever burns deep. I'm afraid to move him from the hold."

I pulled the leg of my pants over my calf and showed him the scars. "She cured me of this, I think she can help your friend."

"I'm sure there's a story there," he said and got up to leave.

I followed him from the cabin and watched as he took a bucket of water and some dried turtle down into the hold. Swift had the watch and I went to the helm. "Mason says there's a harbor around that point there."

"Oh, Mason says, does he?"

I knew he was worried about losing power to the newcomer. "You've got a share of everything larger than he even knows. If he's got value, especially in these waters, we need to use him."

"Aye. Any hazards?" he asked.

I pointed toward an area just before the tip of the island. "He says there's some shallows and to give it some leeway as you go around. I'll wake Syd to help with the sails."

Mason and Syd were both on deck and I decided to trust the newcomer at the helm. Swift reluctantly turned over the wheel, after I recounted the man's knowledge of the area and the three of us went to work the sails. "Need a lead?" I asked.

"No. I've been here. Might take down a bit of canvas though. It'll be close quarters when we round the bend."

We dropped the foresails into their lazyjacks, lashed them down and climbed the main mast to release the topsail. We were still moving fast, I guessed at seven knots and remembered what he had said about the current. Now that it was working in our favor we were making the same speed as the opposite direction with less than half the sail.

"Prepare to come about," he called as he cut the wheel to starboard.

We moved forward and watched the sails swing to port where they caught the wind. He called orders to release the jibs and spill some air from the mainsail as we hugged the northern bank and made for the half dozen shacks ahead. A hundred yards out he called to drop the main and we crept forward

"Drop the anchor," he called as we slowed to a near stop and he swung the boat into the current.

With a bit of regret I threw the silver ballast overboard, but not before checking the attachment. I did not want to lose this anchor. It held and the boat pulled tight then swung a few degrees with the bow into the current.

"Joshua Appleby," Mason stood at the rail and yelled toward the shacks.

"What the hell is he doing?" Swift asked.

Syd moved his hand to his dagger ready to silence the man. "Let it play out. He's been nothing but honest and without his help, we might be wrecked on the reef."

He relaxed his hand, but it remained on the hilt of the knife.

"He's no better than you," Mason said. "You've no worries here."

A figure appeared on the porch of the closest building. "Joshua. It's Mason. I've got a man in need of attention."

"And the rest? I know that boat. Smugglers and slavers the last I looked," he cupped his hands and yelled back.

"They took the boat from that lot. I suspect you might get along with this bunch. Now would you kindly row out here, we're without a launch."

The four of us stood by the rail as the man rowed to us. A handful of people had gathered on the shore as well, two small enough to be children, but they looked dark skinned and I doubted it was a coincidence.

"Those two," I called down to the man as Mason tossed him a line to secure the boat.

He looked up and growled, "Can you wait a bloody minute."

The boat tipped and I suspected from the way his cheeks showed red in the lantern light that he had been drinking. I decided not to press him. As anxious as I was, I would know soon enough.

He exchanged a few words with Mason and we went to rig a stretcher to haul the man from the hold. Swift found a board and we descended into the darkness. He was still alive, but his skin was red and swollen and I could tell he held heat without touching him. We rolled him onto the board and fashioned a harness to secure him to it. Swift, Syd and I went above to raise him while Mason stayed below to guide the stretcher. He came up easily, and I saw why as the moonlight illuminated his emaciated body.

We swung the boom overboard and started to lower him to the launch.

"Best get a man down there. Your friend Joshua doesn't look too steady on his feet," I said to Mason.

He descended the rope ladder to the launch and signaled that he was ready. Hand over hand we lowered the stretcher to the deck of the waiting boat.

"We'll come back out for you," Mason called as the man released the line and started to row to shore.

"Not that I don't trust them, but something's odd with that group on the shore and I don't mean to wait," I told Syd and Swift before pulling my shirt over my head and diving in the water.

The water was cold, but after a week without bathing, it felt good as the sweat and grime washed from my skin. I swam the distance to the beach and waded onto shore. The two figures came toward me and I knew I was right.

"Mr. Nick," Blue said as he came toward me. Lucy rushed past him and embraced me. "Mr. Nick, bad men come to the island with uniforms. They take Red."

"And what of Rhames?" I looked around hoping my right hand man would show himself.

"Mr. Rhames is in the shack drunk," Lucy said and pointed to a small building.

I went toward it in a fury, wondering what had happened. "Lucy, the man they have in the small boat needs your help," I said as I walked into the shack.

Rhames was prone on a cot, snoring loudly. I smacked his head and waited as he slowly gathered his wits.

"What happened?" I asked.

He looked up and squinted, "Well look at the bloody likes of you. Damn site for sore eyes."

I knew he was still under the influence, but I needed to know what happened to Red and the treasure. "Come on. Snap out of it. Blue said there were men in uniform that took Red."

"Bloody hell, those Navy bastards. They came in the longboats. Old Red was drunk and didn't get to the canoe in time.

He probably wasn't the only drunk one, but I was glad to see Rhames all the same and left him to sleep it off.

Chapter Six

I could tell from the look on Lucy's face that the man was in a bad way. "Doesn't look good," I said as I stood by her side. Sweat poured from his skin and his face was swollen and red. She was hovering over him, washing him with what looked like the same concoction she had used on me.

"No, Mr. Nick. I think it is too late," she said as she worked.

I walked outside and stood by Mason, who was staring at the sky. "She's doing all she can."

He just shrugged and continued to stare.

"I'll be heading back to the ship. We'll stay for the night and see what tomorrow brings."

He acknowledged me with a nod.

I had found the canoe that Rhames, Blue, and Lucy had used to escape the Navy and paddled it back to the boat. I tied it to the line from our ship and climbed the rope ladder hung over the side.

"Might have brought a bit of rum with you," Syd slurred as he tapped the empty keg.

They had been drinking, but as far as I could tell were not quite drunk. "I could use a bit myself, but there are some complications." I told them of the raid on the island, the capture of Red and the escape of the others.

"That's all I know for now. Rhames is passed out and Lucy is working on the man," I said and rose.

"What about Red?" Swift asked about his friend.

"We won't leave him to hang, but we need to find out if he's in a jail cell in Key West or the brig of the frigate. If it's the brig, there's nothing we can do, but he'll be safe until they put ashore. If he's held on land, they could swing him any time."

"Fair enough. Then we leave for Key West?" Syd asked.

"Let me sleep on it." I walked away. Back in my cabin I laid out on the bunk and started to think. Although Red was a constant thorn in my side, he was part of my crew. Despite any feelings I had about him, if the Navy had not already found our treasure, he knew where it was. I did not want him to use its location as a bargaining chip to negotiate for his freedom, or let them torture it out of him. One way or another we had to rescue him.

The wind woke me late in the night and I cursed myself for falling asleep without assigning a watch. I rubbed my eyes and swung my feet onto the deck. The boat was bobbing like a cork in a pool and the wind was whistling through the rigging. I left the cabin, climbed the stairs onto the deck and walked toward the bow.

Whitecaps topped the small wind-blown waves in the harbor and although I couldn't see the open water, I knew from the wind that the seas would be higher than my head. I turned back to shore and was surprised to see lanterns lit in the cabins. I moved back to the companionway and yelled down for Swift and Syd to wake up.

A few minutes later they joined me on deck and we watched the activity on land as several figures were preparing the schooner for sea. The boat was similar to ours in rigging, but was beamier to accommodate more in its holds. The men were talking, but the wind was in my face and I couldn't make out what they were saying. I suspected we were not in danger. If they had wanted, they could have snuck onto the boat in the night and slit our throats. A large man staggered out of the shack where I had left Rhames and I struggled to see if it was him. He waved both arms in our direction and yelled, but I couldn't make out his words over the clatter in the rigging.

He cupped his hands together. "Make ready to sail Nick. There's a wreck on the reef," he yelled.

Mason had told me about the men here and called them wreckers, a trade I could only understand as a legal form of pirating. The reef did the work, and although he had said that lives were saved more often than not, the spoils were ill gotten gains. "Right then," I called to Swift and Syd. " Get the boat ready. I'll get Rhames."

I could see their excitement at the prospect of adventure as I climbed over the ladder and swung myself into the canoe. The small craft rocked with the waves and I was careful not to lean over when I released the line. Rhames was waiting when I reached the beach and before I had grounded he waded into the water and spun the boat around before hopping in.

"Wait a minute. Let me check on Mason. He's a good hand and knows how this is done."

He looked at me with that queer look he used when he's not sure what I meant and I realized he didn't know of our discovery of the men in the hold of the ship. I didn't have time to tell him now and stepped into the water, leaving him alone in the canoe. Mason was standing on the end of the pier talking to the man he had introduced as Joshua Appleby. They turned to me as I approached.

"Joshua wants to partner with you. Word is there's a boat wrecked on Sombrero Key," Mason spoke for them. "Says the wreck is too big to salvage with just his boat."

I was not sure about this whole business, or what a partnership involved, but the only way to learn was to take a risk and find out.

"As long as you pilot our ship, you have a deal." I extended my hand to the men.

They looked at each other and nodded. "We leave in ten minutes," Joshua said. "Listen to Mason, son. He knows the trade."

I ignored the insult and ran to the shack where Lucy and Blue were tending the man. I wanted them both onboard, but would settle for Blue if Lucy was still needed here. In calm seas, the boat could be sailed with a handful of men, as we had done, but in heavy seas we would need every able body I could muster. I entered the room and saw Blue in the corner sitting on his haunches.

"We ready, Mr. Nick. Lucy will stay with the man, but I will go," he said and grabbed his tube. Without a word to Lucy he walked past me through the door and into the night.

The four of us would have capsized in the choppy waters so we split and took two shuttles. Once aboard I looked over at the other boat. "Raise the main with two reefs," I ordered, copying what Appleby had done. Rhames and Swift were already in the rigging and unlashed the ties. The sail rose out of the lazyjacks and we started to move.

Tie off the anchor line to the canoe," Mason called to me and winked.

He didn't want the ballast examined and I doubted it would hold in open water anyway. I went forward, took a turn of the line on the winch and pulled enough slack to reach the stern where the tender line was tied to the rail. Braced against the rail to keep slack in the anchor line, I removed the canoe's line and tied a sheet bend, and let them go. We were underway now and I watched Mason turn from the wind to allow the other boat the lead.

The reefed main caught as he steered us back to the wind and we moved forward. Leaving the harbor was easy with the wind at our backs, but as we rounded the point and the sun started to rise I saw the churning water ahead. On days like this, pirates drank rum. But this weather is when wreckers worked and we clung to anything we could as the waves crashed over the bowsprit covering the deck with spray.

We were less than five miles from the reef, and I could see a mast askew on the horizon. Mason called to raise the foresail and we picked up more speed. For the better part of an hour we fought the wind and waves. Finally we came within hailing distance of the wrecked boat and shortened sail. We kept a safe distance and watched Appleby, his boat standing off in deeper water, at the tip of the bowsprit yelling back and forth with a man on the sinking ship. I couldn't make out the words, but expected they were negotiating for the rights to the cargo in exchange for saving the crew. Suddenly the captain broke off the negotiation and looked toward shore. We all turned to follow his gaze and saw two other boats heading toward us.

Appleby yelled back to him and the man appeared to accept his terms as he threw him a line. One of the crew caught it and secured the boats together and the wreck was ours. Mason closed on the boats and my jaw dropped as I stared across the void at the captain who had taken Rory.

Chapter Seven

Appleby's crew ran his launch back and forth removing the men stranded on the wrecked boat and bringing them to his. I scanned the worried faces waiting by the rail looking for Rory, but saw no sign of her.

"That's the boat I put the girl on," I said to Rhames who stood next to me.

He squinted into the sun. "Don't see her now," he said and leaned over to grab the rope a crewman from the launch below us was about to toss up.

Communication was difficult between the boats, but Mason knew what Appleby wanted and we were prepared to receive the line in order to tow the wreck off the reef. He had just returned from evaluating the damage with Appleby and several of his crew. The men had conferred and agreed that in its present state, the boat would be torn apart by the coral before the cargo could be offloaded. Their plan was to tow the boat into deeper water where a temporary repair could be made and the rest of the crew safely evacuated. I had to admit that although fascinated by the process, quite a bit of what he said was lost on me as we had more experience sinking boats than saving them.

The boats were drifting apart. Rhames grabbed the line and took a few turns around the winch used to raise the anchor. The mechanical advantage provided by the winch took some of the load off the line allowing us to gain enough slack to tie it off. Appleby was in the process of fixing another line to his stern. He signaled to us and we followed as he changed his course to keep the boats parallel. We followed suit as he raised his mainsail. Mason yelled from the helm to stay clear as the tow line became taut, shedding a spray of water on the deck as it stretched. The boats stalled and again we followed Appleby's lead as he raised his topsails. With the additional canvas, the tension in the line felt like it was about to tear apart our boat and I looked for the ax in case we needed to cut it. The entire boat shook and groaned, but finally began to move. I looked back and saw the wreck shift and then follow us into deeper water. Now that it was free we continued what I guessed was a quarter mile before dropping our sails.

Both boats had all hands pulling the wreck toward us using the tow lines and winches. When the wreck was within a hundred feet, Appleby gave the command to tie off the lines. We were drifting together, but the water was deep and he dropped his anchor before turning his attention to the sinking ship.

I had nothing to do but watch and hope that Rory would appear. Since she had boarded the boat her screams still echoed in my head and hadn't been far from my thoughts since we had escaped the harbor in Key West. I couldn't wait any longer to see if she was still aboard and jumped over the rail. The waves battered me as I swam toward the foundering ship and I struggled to keep my head above the water as several large swells tried to submerge me. I reached the boat, swam to a section of rigging lying in the water from the downed foremast and used it to haul myself aboard. The deck was a flurry of activity as Appleby's men worked to keep the boat afloat.

I looked around and didn't see her, and the captain stared at me with a malicious grin on his face as he went over the side with the last of his crew. I looked down into the hold and saw much of the cargo floating in the building water. The companionway was aft of the hold and I went to it, hoping the damage was to the hold and the cabins would be free of water.

I descended the ladder to the living compartments and found myself in knee deep water in the galley, its entire contents floating in the water around me. "Rory," I yelled several times as I moved toward the crew cabins. There were no doors on either and both were empty. I yelled her name again and moved back through the galley, noticing the water was higher on my legs than when I first entered. The door to the captain's cabin was ajar and I called her name again before entering. It was empty as well and I feared I would have to go into the hold.

I climbed the companionway stairs two at a time and reached the deck. Four men were gathering the fallen mainsail and called for my help, but I kept moving toward the hold. The water was high here that it was not worth using the ladder and I jumped blindly into the darkness. Chest deep in water I swam forward toward the hatch leading to the forward hold, the same compartment where I had found Mason and his men on our ship. I reached it and tugged on the door, but it wouldn't move. I called her name again, and this time thought I heard a response, but the water pouring in around me was too loud to be certain.

A timber floated by and I reached for it. Barely able to stand, I grasped the board and butted it into the door. Wood splintered and I hit it several more times creating a hole large enough to crawl through. I released the board and squirmed through the hole, trying to avoid the jagged edges of the shattered wood. I gained my footing and looked around. It was dark inside but I saw movement off in a corner.

"Rory," I yelled and was sure I heard a voice in return. This hold had not been damaged by the reef and held half the water of the main hold, but with the hatch broken, the water flowed in freely.

"Over here," she called.

I found her in the same position as the men aboard the ship we had taken, her wrists and ankles manacled to the hull. Furious she had been left to die, I found a loose bar and pried the restraints from the deck.

"Well. Look who it is. My favorite pirate saving me again," she said as she rose slowly.

"We have to get out of here," I grabbed her arm and pushed her ahead of me toward the door. "Can you get through the hole?"

She laughed and launched herself through the opening, able to swim through as the water continued to rise. I followed and guided her to the cargo rope hanging from the boom above. I climbed first and then hauled her onto the deck where she sat.

"Can you give us a hand here mate?" one of the men working the downed sail called.

I looked at Rory and she nodded. The men were rolling the mainsail, its length parallel with the rail. Two lines long enough to reach around the hull were stretched out by it. A crewman took one end and went forward to the bowsprit where he passed it under the strut. Another man was there to grab the end and with one man on the starboard rail and the other the port they walked the line stretched under the boat until they reached the stern end of the boat. Another man called for me to help him do the same and we stretched a second line below the damaged section of the hull.

The bitter ends of the starboard lines were tied to the rail and the ends of the lines on the port side were tied to the sail. We hauled on the starboard lines while two men fed the sail overboard stretching it under the hull. It was hard work and the crew was tense as we tried to keep it tight against the boat. If we allowed it to fill with water, the weight could pull us to the bottom of the sea. I looked at the water below and saw the edge of the sail was now visible above the water on our side. I followed the other mens lead and tied the lines off. With the patch finally in place we caught our breath and waited to see if it would take hold.

"Man the pumps," the lead man called out.

Several men jumped into the hold and water soon shot out of the thru-hull fittings high on the sides of the boat. After a few minutes the rest of us jumped in and spelled them. I was surprised to find the water only knee deep as I took the handle and started to pump. By the time I tired the water was ankle deep and we relaxed, exchanging grins.

Rory was still on deck where I had left her when I climbed out covered in sweat.

"Are you alright?" I asked as I approached her.

"Fine ship you sold me to."

I ignored the barb and reached down for her. She took my hand and we fell into a tight embrace. I could feel her chest heave and the warmth of her tears on my chest and let her cry until she was done. Finally she looked up at me. "Thank you."

Chapter Eight

We had to work in shifts to man the pumps and keep the ship afloat. On a break, I had inspected the patch made from draping the sail over the damaged hull and although it held, the pressure of the sea behind it forced water through the porous material. The boat wasn't sinking, but it didn't look like it could be repaired. Appleby had towed her to deeper water and she was anchored now, just off the reef in what looked to be thirty feet of water, listing sadly to port. Our vessel was tied off to Appleby's boat as we had no anchor of our own.

The deck was a flurry of activity as the day wore on and the men, including myself took turns at the pumps to keep the wreck afloat, while others worked to remove her cargo from the holds. The seas had settled as the hours passed, but there was an urgency in our work. I wiped the sweat from my brow and looked over at our ship.

Rory had been shuttled over by one of the launches hours ago and I wondered how she fared. She had been beaten and abused over the two days since we had parted. I felt responsible for her treatment, even though she had insisted on boarding the boat. In her anger with us and haste to leave she had made a bad decision. I had noticed her staring intently toward Appleby's boat, looking for a sign of the captain. He had been invisible, hiding ever since he had seen me bring her to daylight, a smart move. If I knew anything about her, those that crossed her paid dearly as I had seen with the trader on the Caloosahatchee.

It was my turn for a break and I sat by the rail drinking water from a tin cup. Mason and Syd approached and sat by me.

"We need to go talk to Appleby and negotiate our share," Mason said.

I was tired. "Can't it wait until we get back to land?"

"It'll be best now. We left as partners and there's decisions to be made."

I looked at him, unsure of what he meant.

"The fate of the boat and cargo for starters. He negotiated a deal with the captain of the wreck before we offloaded her crew, and we need to find out the terms. We left his dock as equals and I know the man well enough, but if he means to burn the wreck we need to take our share now."

"Burn it?"

"That's the way it works. If we leave it here, it'll signal other boats where the reef is, at least until the sea claims her." he said.

Syd smiled, "Sounds a bit like pirating after all."

It did, but I knew the laws of the sea gave us a legal right to the boat and cargo. The Bahamians had set up a court to hear cases and distribute salvage, and I expected the United States would follow. But for now, it was fair game to negotiate with the captain.

A launch called from below to throw a line and we helped them tie off. After the men climbed aboard, we took the boat to Appleby's ship.

He leaned over the rail as we climbed the ladder. "I was expecting you hours ago."

We stood in a half circle, watching the activity on the wreck. The cargo was piled high on the deck waiting to be offloaded.

"We had a deal to work as partners," I started. "What do you intend for the cargo and boat?"

"The boat we've got to burn. I had a look earlier and there's no repairing the damage the reef caused her." He pulled a pipe from his pocket and struck a match against his boot sole. "As for the cargo," He inhaled and paused before blowing a cloud of smoke toward me. "As for the cargo, we each take a share, but it's my deal and I'll take first pick."

"And what of the captain and crew," I asked more interested in Rory than the cargo.

"What of them?" He inhaled again and I waited for him to continue. "We bring them to land and they fend for themselves. If they've got some gold, we can take them to Key West."

"The cargo seems fair. But the captain needs to face justice for what he's done to the girl," I said and told him the story of her desire to find a ship home, negotiating her passage with the captain and her subsequent abuse.

"What about Red?" Syd asked.

I hadn't thought about him. We needed to help Red before he divulged the location of the treasure and Key West was the logical place to look for him. But, that harbor had not proven friendly to me on the last visit.

"You can have first pick of the cargo, but you'll need to dispose of the captain and crew," I said. The last thing I needed was the captain anywhere near Rory after watching what she did to the trader.

"If that's what you want young captain," he puffed again.

"Let's get on with it," I said, sure I had cut a bad deal, but anxious to find Red.

He called orders to his men and we boarded the launch to go back to the wreck and divide the cargo.

It took the rest of the afternoon to split the goods and shuttle them to our boats. I wasn't all that impressed if this is what wrecking was about. It seemed a lot of work for the goods involved, but I guess some ships were richer than others. It had been the same gamble when we were pirating.

We retrieved the wreck's anchor to replace the one we had lost and almost capsized as we pushed to escape the fire that Appleby's men had just lit. The tether tying us to Appleby's boat was released just as the sun set and I looked behind at the boat burning bright in the sky behind us. The entire vessel was engulfed in flame and with the masts down it looked like a fire on the water.

We followed Appleby back to the harbor and tossed out the new anchor into the shallow water. Exhausted we lay on the deck talking about the day when Rory appeared.

"What about the captain. I'll do him justice right now."

She had cleaned up and replaced her torn and blood stained dress with a sailor's clothes she had found below. The bruises on her face were still visible in the lantern light and I wondered how badly they had treated her. "He'll get justice," I assured her, although I had no reason to believe Appleby would do anything of the sort if the captain could buy his way from captivity.

This seemed to appease her and I was glad for it as I was too tired for a fight. My only thought was how to get in and out of the island without using the harbor. We couldn't take the chance of being seen by the Navy.

"And, I'll be looking for another boat home," she said.

I bit the words back as I was about to say that she ought to be a bit more patient and chose a better ship this time, but left it unsaid. "Join us for a bit of rum?"

She took the offered cup and stood by the rail, staring at the water. "How is the man you saved?"

We sat together and I told her of Mason and the other man as we sailed back from the reef. It was dark when we reached the anchorage and the men, except for Blue, collapsed on deck. He was anxious to see Lucy and paddled the canoe to the shacks.

We sat in the same place, just about asleep when he returned.

"Mr. Nick, the man, he died this morning." Lucy said. "It was too late when I got to him."

I got up and stood next to her at the rail. There was a lantern burning by itself off to the side of the small village where I guessed they were burying him.

"I'm going to shore," I told her. I need to have some words with Mason and Appleby before we leave tomorrow," I watched the lantern move back to the shacks, several figures following behind it. "That man Mason knows these waters and would be a good addition to our crew."

"And what are you going to do once you leave Key West? Is it back to pirating?"

I had been thinking about that and knew there was no future in the trade. "Those days are behind us," I said thinking about the silver in the hold and fascinated by Masons talk of breathing underwater. "Maybe we'll try something different."

Chapter Nine

It took until late the next afternoon to split the cargo and make some necessary repairs to the ship. I made a deal with Appleby, trading him a good portion of the haul for one of his launches. We had enough silver in the bilge and treasure buried on the island that I wasn't worried about the cost. He had been into the rum and wanted to gamble for it, feeling rich himself after the wreck, but I declined. My expertise in games of risk was only less than my luck. Rhames had offered to play in my place but the wrecker declined the more experienced man.

Rory was anxious to leave, but slept most of the day in my cabin. She rose around dusk, asked when we would be leaving and went back to bed. Rhames caught me staring out the entrance to the harbor as the sun set.

"I imagine you have a plan to rescue Red?" he asked.

I watched the incoming tide rush against the hull, waiting for it to change so we could raise anchor. "The captain of the Navy frigate will know our boat if he's in the harbor. There are two small keys that should conceal us. I saw them when we were coming through the passage from the Gulf. We can anchor there and take the launch to shore. The only one there that knows my face is the harbormaster and a few coins should keep his mouth shut. We can leave a few men to guard the boat and have a look around. I mean to find Red before they hang him."

"Poor bastard's probably shit his pants. That one is all talk and when they put the screws to him I hope he shuts his trap," Rhames said.

"I had the same feeling. Better to get to him quickly."

***

Rhames woke the crew as soon as the tide changed. The moon was high and waxing near full, the cloud cover opaque, but did little to temper the light. We all knew our duties and I put Mason at the helm as he knew the waters better than the rest of us. Rhames and Syd went into the rigging while Swift, Blue, and I hauled on the anchor rode and dragged the chain around the winch. As soon as the men raised the mainsail, we hauled the anchor off the sandy bottom and stowed it. The tide started to move the boat in the direction of the entrance and under the mainsail we passed through the mouth of the harbor and into open water.

The sea sparkled in the predawn hours with the moon reflecting off the small waves. The wind continued to blow from the northeast, but was a light breeze now. From our days at sea I knew that times like this were rare. Out of a fortnight on the water, two days might be like this, two would have the men leaning over the rails emptying their stomachs and the rest would be somewhere in between. I was able to relax with Rhames and Mason onboard, both better sailors than I.

Around dawn Rory came on deck and sat by me. "Penny for your thoughts."

"I'd give a gold piece for yours," I countered. This drew a spell of silence, but she finally relented.

"Were you serious about swearing off the pirate life?" she asked.

I wasn't sure where this was going but answered honestly. "I was never really a pirate, but abducted like you."

"I know, but you let the crew murder those men back at the river."

"I'm in a bit of a tenuous position. They trust me for my brain, not my brawn. I can't fight like them and can only watch when the bloodlust strikes." I felt awkward telling her my weakness, but it was the truth. When the men got that look in their eyes I could only stand back and watch.

"This man Mason, he seems more like you."

A wave of jealousy passed through me, and I waited to respond. "He's told me of this equipment that lets a man breathe underwater."

"What's that got to do with anything?"

"We've got a taste of wrecking now and with the Navy prowling around, there's no future in pirating. It's kind of like looting a ship, but they need your help."

"So you intend to be a wrecker?" she asked

"Something to think about. But from what Mason has told me with many of these shipwrecks the heavier cargo often finds its way to the bottom. Treasure fleets have been running these waters for hundreds of years." I leaned back and looked at the stars dreaming about finding one of the old Spanish armadas loaded with the wealth of the lower Americas.

We sat in silence for a while and watched the sun come up. Key West would be about six hours ahead if I guessed our speed correctly. I needed to know her aim before we reached port. "Are you still planning on seeking out a ship?"

She sat and stared at the deck. "It's crossed my mind that I might be safer not rushing into things."

My heart leapt in my chest and I tried to hide my excitement.

"Well, Lucy would be happy for the company."

"And not you?" she leaned closer.

We sat that way, watching the waves until Mason called from the helm.

"It's your watch," he called to me.

I moved slightly and realized she was fast asleep. As gently as I could I eased her against the bulkhead and went to the wheel.

"You need to learn to sail this craft of yours," he said and moved from the wheel. For the next two hours he coached me, teaching the nuances of riding waves and staying on course. Before I knew it, the mass of Key West loomed in the distance and he asked my plan.

"We need to make a run in the deeper water past the entrance to the harbor and hope the frigate's not watching. There are two islands off the coast a bit. I mean to anchor in between them."

"You know what kind of water you're talking about? I know the spot. It may look deep to the eye, but that's the turtle grass darkening the water and making it look deeper than it is. Hold the course, I'll be back," he said, went to the companionway and disappeared.

A few minutes later he emerged with a lead and held it out to me. "It's wax melted on it," he said.

I looked confused and he continued. "The wax will tell you what kind of bottom you're in." He went forward and dropped the wax coated weight. A few seconds later he pulled in the line and brought the weight to me. Sand coated the wax. "See that. Hard bottom. It'll come in handy up ahead.

I got all hands on deck as we reached the Key and stayed at the wheel with Mason behind me. I called orders to trim the sails as I turned close to ninety degrees and headed north. I wanted as much speed as she could muster as we passed the mouth of the harbor and I wasn't disappointed as the boat groaned under the load of the wind and heeled over. In less than a minute we were past the entrance, hopefully unseen.

Mason took the lead to Syd and had him toss it as the rest of the crew dropped the sails leaving only the main and prepared to anchor. Syd called out the depths and bottom as we approached the gap between the islands. As soon as he called mud, I knew we were in the grass and ordered the anchor dropped.

Chapter Ten

I wasted no time in getting the boat prepared for a quick escape in the event we needed to make a hasty exit. It was near dark when we pulled in the painter and Mason and I climbed the ladder down to the canoe. Without a word, I released the line and sat facing forward as we began our paddle toward the gulf side of the harbor entrance. We had decided the two of us would go alone as the rest of the crew was more well known. Lucy and Rory had shaved Rhames head and beard, and I had to admit his mother would have a hard time recognizing him, but I needed him in charge of the boat if something should happen. Despite being hidden between the islands, there was still enough boat traffic, mainly fishermen seeking turtles, that there was a chance we would be noticed.

We reached a beach on the north side of the point leading into the harbor and dragged the canoe ashore. After hauling it to the line of palm trees and brush we used some downed branches to conceal it. It wouldn't stand a hard look, but in the fading light it should suffice as I planned to be back aboard the boat before the moon rose. Fighting the mosquitos and brush we set out on foot to cross the small peninsula and scout out the harbor. A few minutes later we could see lights from lanterns marking the houses. I strained for a look into the harbor to see if the frigate was there, but it was too dark. Mason led, claiming knowledge of the layout of the small village and I followed.

A small shack bordered the woods and we stopped to look and listen for any sign of its occupants before setting foot into the cluttered clearing behind the house. We moved slowly around the piles of turtle shells until we reached the back of the house. It was covered with weathered rough sawn boards running vertically and had a thatched roof. There were two mismatched windows and a small chimney, more for cooking than heat, ran through the roof. The interior was dark and we could find no sign of life as we made our way around it and onto the street. From what I remembered of London, this was more a path than a street, wide enough for a cart and rutted from the heavy rains. We stayed to the side as we walked toward a cluster of lights near the water that marked the main settlement.

"The jail would be there," Mason pointed at a dark building with bars on the back windows.

The building appeared to have been hastily constructed and leaned slightly to one side, but was sturdy, built with what looked to be white-washed brick construction with a wooden roof. The front of the building had a small porch and a room which I guessed belonged to whatever law enforcement the small village had. We stayed in the shadows until we reached the back of the building. The window was too high to see through but except for the bars was open to the air. From inside I could hear snoring.

"Red," I whispered and waited but the snoring continued. I picked up several small pieces of broken bricks laying nearby and tossed one in the opening. Still the snoring continued, but after several more pieces, each larger than the last, the noise stopped and I could hear someone move inside. "Red," I called again.

"Nick, is that you?" the voice came back loud enough to make me cringe and check the street to see if anyone had heard.

"Quiet now. Are you alright?" I whispered.

"Aye. Bastards have got nothing out of me," he said, his voice lower.

"Good. What do they intend?"

"You know this lot. Can't string you up without a trial. It's the Americans, you know. If it was the bloody Spanish, the crabs would be eating my guts by now."

"Did they tell you when the trial is?" I said.

"The best I can tell, they're waiting for the frigate to come back. A lawyer, they promised me. Said it was in their Constitution. Silly bastards."

I breathed a sigh of relief. He was right, two months ago when the island had been in Spanish hands, he would have been tortured for what he knew and hung immediately. I looked carefully at the construction of the building. It suffered from poor workmanship, but was substantial enough to be secure. It would take some tools or a bit of powder to breach it. There was no guard as we were isolated on the island where an escaped prisoner would have few choices of where to hide, and there was no way off the Key itself without passing through the town.

"Hang in there mate," I said to reassure him. "Tomorrow night or the next at the latest, we'll be back and spring you."

"Aye, Nick. I knew you was a good man."

We exchanged a few more words on the status of the crew, but I was wary of staying too long. The moon would be full tonight and I wanted to be back aboard the boat before its light hit the water. We still had a few hours to scout the harbor and return to the boat. If the frigate was there I intended to pull anchor and find a safer mooring.

As we approached the pier, we heard voices coming from a

building I guessed to be a makeshift bar along the main street. There were two or three buildings large enough to house a business, though none were marked. Mason and I stayed clear of the bar, went around the back of the harbormaster's shack and stood on the end of the pier where we had an unobstructed view of the harbor. There were several large boats at anchor and a dozen or so fishing boats, often tied three deep against the pier.

"I don't see the frigate," I said.

"No, but there's a few boats here that I would take care to avoid," he said.

"I've seen enough. Let's get back to the ship and make a plan to spring Red." I turned to walk away but stopped as I heard voices nearby. "Quick, behind the building."

We reached the back of the building just as two men entered the office and light spilled from the window as a lantern was lit. I slid over to the side of the open window anxious for news.

"You're the agent for Warner and Mountain?"

"Names Greene. Colonel P.C. Green at your service. And you represent Simonton and Whitehead?" I recognized the gruff tone of the harbormaster.

"That's right. Seems they're interested in how you came to be running this spit of land as your bosses only own twenty-five percent."

I could smell the tobacco as the harbormaster lit his pipe. "Seems you're a bit misinformed. I've been here since before the Spanish. Just keeping order and collecting rents is all."

"Well Simonton and Whitehead will be looking for an accounting," the stranger said.

"I've got it here. Let me just open the safe."

The room was silent for a moment until the stranger spoke. "You haven't seen or heard of any of Gasparilla's lot, have you?"

"Why do you ask?" the harbormaster replied.

I chanced a look in the window and saw him rise from the safe with a large ledger, his hand holding something underneath it.

"Seems there was couple of longboats and empty chests that floated out of the Caloosahatchee river. The lot of it just floated into the bay after the last storm."

I had a moment of panic and turned away from the scene in the room. The two longboats and empty chests we had left under the brush by the river had been a long way from the water level, but a storm the size of what we had experienced in the river of grass could easily have raised the water level enough to float the boats out of the depression. I cursed under my breath for not scuttling them, but was interrupted by a gunshot and turned back toward the window.

The stranger was prone on the floor, blood pooling around him, the harbormaster standing over him with his pipe in his mouth and a pistol in his hand. Mason grabbed my arm and pulled me into the shadows as the door opened and we watched the harbormaster haul the body to the edge of the dock and push it in the water. The light extinguished and we could hear the sound of the safe closing. He emerged a few minutes later, closed the door and walked down the pier where he turned inland onto the street leading to the brig.

I left the cover of the building with Mason behind me. We made sure the harbormaster was out of sight before we took off at a run on the trail that lead toward the shack that led to the trail. The brush cut us and we both tripped several times as we fought our way to the beach where we had left the boat, uncovered it and hauled it to the water. We didn't speak until we were half way to our ship.

"It's gotta be tonight. That bastard Greene is on his way to get what he can out of Red," I said.

He looked at me as if I spoke a different language.

"Well you knew we were pirates. Those were our boats and chests the stranger was talking about."

Chapter Eleven

"Gather the guns and swords. We could use some powder as well," I yelled to the startled crew as my feet hit the deck. "We need to get Red now." I went to the group who were gathered around the companionway. "Somehow, the boats and chests that we stashed along the river floated free in the storm and made their way to the Gulf. We overheard someone in the harbormaster's office tell him about it."

They looked at each other, knowing that if Red talked, out treasure was in jeopardy. We had the option to pull anchor and retrieve the treasure now, but I determined the best course of action was to rescue Red before he told them about us or the treasure. It fit my plans to remain anonymous and put our pirate reputation behind us.

"You heard him," Rhames broke the spell, a large grin on his face.

The men dispersed leaving Rory and Mason staring at me.

"I thought you were through with pirating and murder," Rory said.

I paused and thought about how to respond, knowing I had to be careful with my words as she would twist them like a barrister, "This has nothing to do with murder and pirating. In fact it's quite the opposite. If Red talks, they will know the boat and who is on it. We will be marked men. By freeing him, we can put the past behind us." That seemed to satisfy her and I turned to Mason, "I know this is not your business. You are welcome to stay aboard with Rory, Lucy and Blue."

"What makes you think I'm staying aboard?" Rory asked.

"I just assumed …"

"That I'd trust you lot of thieving bastards with my portion of the treasure. Well think again. I'll be going to protect my interests," She said and disappeared down the stairs.

The men were assembled by the starboard rail, weapons in hand. "Load into the launch," I ordered. "I'll be right behind you."

I watched as they started to go over the rail and climb down into the waiting boat before I slid down the ladder to the hold and started moving boxes. Towards the back I uncovered a keg full of black powder. With no other supplies to make a charge, I grabbed the empty water bucket, filled it halfway, and went back to the deck where Rory was waiting, a sword by her side and rifle in her hand. I held up a hand to wait and went to the foremast for the ax. Even though it was broken from striking the anchor chain, it might serve us. The other men were already drifting free in the launch as we descended the rope ladder to the canoe. We each grabbed a paddle and set out toward the shore where Mason and I had beached the boats earlier. I looked back to see Mason, Lucy and Blue watching from the rail.

We had to struggle to keep up with the faster launch. "Rhames," I called and he turned his head. "The spots over there. Let me take the lead." He slowed their pace and Rory and I, both breathing hard, moved in front of them. Together we made our way to the small beach, hid the boats and stood in a circle by the brush.

"There's a fisherman's shack through here and then a path to the town. There wasn't much activity before, and its past midnight now,"

I looked up at the full moon just above the horizon, already bright enough to cast shadows. "Syd, you and Swift will stand guard at the shack to cover our retreat. I'll take Rory and Rhames with me.

I led the group through the brush and we emerged behind the shack. It was still dark, and I was sure at this hour the occupants were asleep. "Post the watch here," I pointed to a stack of turtle shells that would conceal the men, but at the same time give them a clear view of anyone coming after us if things went badly. Syd and Swift took their positions and I led Rory and Rhames down the street toward the brig. They both held rifles at the ready and I felt out of place walking with the bucket of powder in one hand and the broken ax in the other. We stopped a block away from the white-washed building. Light from a lantern spilled from a window and I could hear a loud voice coming from inside.

"Rhames, go have a look." I whispered to him and pulled Rory into the shadows of a large gum tree where we watched him approach. I had sent him for his stealth as well as his tactical mind.

He returned a few minutes later. "The bastard's putting the screws to him, but from what I heard he hasn't told him anything."

"Is he in good enough shape to walk?"

"Aye, but if we leave him much longer he might not be. The bastard's pressing him hard," Rhames said.

I stared at the building, waiting for a plan to form in my mind. We heard a scream followed by a whimper and I knew we had run out of time. The pressure of having Rory there was not lost on me. If it were just Rhames with me, I could have sent him in to kill the harbormaster, but now we would have to use another means to rescue Red. I looked down at the bucket by my feet and realized that without a fuse it was worthless to create an explosion, but by itself it might create a diversion. If we could lure the harbormaster from his interrogation we might be able to grab Red and get away unseen. Whatever happened it was paramount that we not be identified. If he saw us he would recognize Rory and I, and remember what boat we sailed.

"We need a diversion. You and Rory go behind the building. Watch for the flare. When he comes out to look, you can sneak in behind him and get Red. Don't wait for me."

They nodded that they understood and I waited while they got in position. I picked up the bucket and snuck toward the front of the building. There was no place to conceal myself, but I thought if he did see me - a young man wandering the street carrying a bucket and ax, would not cause alarm. High in the trees the breeze was starting to move the palm fronds and I hoped it would not interfere with my plan. I got as close to the door of the brig as I dared and started dumping a steady stream of powder onto the street working in the direction of the pier. When the bucket was empty I tossed it aside and found a position near the midpoint of the path of powder concealed from the building.

I knelt down, took the flint from my pocket, and withdrew my knife. The wind was still blowing through the trees, but I could hardly feel it as I struck the flint with the back of the blade about an inch over the powder. Sparks flew from the stone, and the powder smoldered but didn't catch. I moved some into a pile with my hands and struck again. This time the sparks caught and I was blinded by the flash as the powder flared. I stood up, still unable to see and ran toward the brig.

"Fire!" I yelled as I passed the door and looked behind me to make sure the flames still burned. I yelled again to make sure the harbormaster heard me, for I only had moments before the powder burned out. Black powder will burn bright and hot but its effects are short-lived. "Fire!" I yelled again and ran toward the brush. The harbormaster ran onto the street in a panic, leaving the door open behind him. He ran toward the pier yelling for help as he went. I watched the building as Rhames snuck in behind him and emerged a minute later with Red.

He was hurt and hung onto Rhames and Rory, unable to walk. I left the brush, handed my ax to Rory and took her place under his arm. The fire was already dying out as we moved behind the fisherman's house and entered the brush. Syd and Swift waited to see if anyone pursued us. They joined us a few minutes later as we struggled to haul the injured man through the thick limbs and branches. We moved as fast as we could and emerged on the beach. As we pulled the boats into the water we could hear cries from the village that didn't appear to have anything to do with fire.

Chapter Twelve

We reached the ship and scurried aboard. Rhames was on the ladder directly below Red, using his bulk to push him from below to help him reach the deck. Swift and Syd reached over the gunwale and pulled him aboard. I was last and when I reached the deck I went for the rigging and climbed to get a better view. From where we had anchored, I couldn't see the harbor itself, but lights were visible and I could hear ships being readied to sail. The harbormaster knew that Red had knowledge of the treasure and was not going to let him slip from his grasp.

"Raise anchor," I called out and looked over the water, thankful now for the full moon. We would have a good head-start and although the moon lit the sky, I doubted it would be enough light to reveal us. Mason and Rhames came to the helm.

The three of us huddled around the wheel as the other men prepared the ship for sea. "He's not going to let us go without a fight."

"Aye. We should head to the island and get the treasure," Rhames said.

I paused for a minute and heard the clatter the chain makes when an anchor is being raised. "We don't have enough of a lead. If they even see the direction we are heading they can catch us when we anchor. There's no where else to hide there. Even if we turned toward New Orleans and lost them on the seas we would still be fugitives. We can't let them see the boat or know it was us that took Red."

Rhames nodded. "Aye, but the frigate is up the other coast."

"That leaves only Cuba or the Bahamas," Mason interjected.

We had pirated in both waters with Gasparilla and I thought through the merits of each. But first we needed to get underway and make our escape. Regardless of our destination, we would need the deeper water of the Florida Straights. "Mason, take her out to deep water. I'll give a new heading shortly."

I left the helm to him and pushed Rhames toward the bow. Before I could tell him my plan, Rory came toward us. I had hoped to be well toward a destination before having to deal with her, but here she was.

"And what do you have in mind?" she asked.

"First I need to know if you are with us or against us," I said and glanced at Rhames seeking his approval.

"I'd be curious as to what you're thinking before I say."

We were interrupted by a call from high in the rigging. The sails had caught the breeze and Mason was steering toward deeper water.

"Boat leaving the harbor," Syd called down. "We keep this course we'll be seeing who it is soon enough.

I caught his meaning and wasted no time in laying out my argument. I had already decided on our course and the approaching boat made the decision easier to explain. "Cuba," I said and let the word settle for a minute. I caught the faintest smile on Rhames lips and before Rory could start an argument, I continued. "If we head toward Cuba we have the advantage of leaving both boats behind.

Heading to the Bahamas leaves us no options but the American coast. But, should things not be to our liking in Cuba, we still have the option of riding the gulfstream to the Bahamas."

"But the Bahamas are British," Rory said.

I expected this argument knowing she would feel safer amongst her own. "If we take the risk of running that course, we have to deal with the ship here and possibly the naval frigate." I breathed in hoping she was convinced.

From the look on her face she wasn't sold. "And what do you have planned in Cuba?"

Again I was ready. "What we need is some time to change the boat up a bit. There are some islands off the coast where we can careen the ship and have a look at her hull. She's a common design. We paint her a different color and rename her and the Navy won't know its us that crossed her bow in the harbor last week."

"Captain makes sense," Rhames said.

She looked at him. "If we can disguise the boat as well as we've done for him, it will give us options."

"Options is good," Rhames said.

"So we are settled then," I said and left them to tell Mason of our destination. I couldn't help but notice the sky. Though I was schooled in poetry and philosophy, I had rarely thought about either in my years with the pirates. But now, as I looked around I couldn't help but think about the poetic justice of the moon setting and sun rising in unison, as if our past was behind us and our future ahead. A future I was not certain of, but as the stoics said, there is nothing in this life that is certain and the man that realizes his circumstance may change at any time, will be a happy man, something I wished I could express to the crew as we moved away from the treasure buried on the island.

"Cuba," I told Mason as I reached the helm.

He nodded but did not change course and I had to assume he understood our situation. "We need a secluded spot we can careen the boat and inspect the hull. We give her a new paint job, change up the rigging a little, and she'll look like a different boat."

He looked up in the rigging, inspecting the set of the sails. "I know a few spots that might work. I'd be interested in your plans after that," he said.

"I'd be interested in talking to you more about this diving and wrecking business," I said and could tell from the smile on his face that he was interested. I left him and went to the rail where I looked out at the sea.

Birds were crashing the bait in the water in front of us and I wondered if there was a hand-line below that I could set out and catch some of the larger fish sure to be below the bait. "We can talk later, but if you're not interested we can drop you in Havana."

He nodded and I went forward to the companionway, climbed down the small flight of steps and entered the galley. Lucy and Blue were sitting at the table, I told them of our destination, and went in search of fishing gear. There were two hand-spools in a locker and I noticed Blue looking at me. I nodded to him and we went on deck together. We each stood on a corner of the transom. Tied to the end of each line was a silver spoon, a feather draped over it concealing the hook, that went into the water as we unwound the line behind it.

The birds were just in front of us now as the spoons floated behind the boat, its momentum pulling them forward to look like baitfish. I showed him how to wrap a small section around his arm to give the fish a bit of slack when it hit, but in the middle of my demonstration the line jerked from both our hands at once. Fortunately we had tied the ends to the rail or we would have lost both rigs as the fish pulled and the line snapped from our hands.

Two fish jumped in unison about a hundred feet behind the boat and I yelled to Mason to veer off the wind slightly. If they were as large as they appeared it would make it easier to bring them in. The rest of the group were soon gathered around offering help and encouragement. Blue refused the help, but I had dealt with many fish and took the offer. If he indeed wanted to enjoy the sport and bring in his fish alone, we would need to get mine aboard fast to keep it from tangling the lines.

I saw the smile on his face as he played it and decided that even if he lost the fish, this was something he sorely needed and if he did lose it, fish in these waters were plentiful. Syd and Swift were by my side as we alternated pulling my line in. Soon the dolphin fish was at the transom, but with this kind of fish the fight was just beginning. I guessed it to be thirty pounds or so as the length looked to be around four feet as it followed the boat trying to regain its strength.

"Get the ax," I called out as the three of us started to haul the fish over the transom. Rory returned with the broken blade and I took it from her as soon as the fish hit the deck. I paused for a second to admire the dolphin fish. During a fight, they are something to behold as they reflect the mood of the fish during the fight, from a deep green when it relaxed to brilliant silvers and blues when it was excited. The fish slammed its body against the wood, its powerful form moving anything in its way. It slowed for a second and I took a swing at its head but missed, splintering the deck boards with the broken blade. The fish sensed the blow and fought even harder now. The deck was slippery with blood from the flailing fish as I wound up to strike again, this time connecting.

We turned our attention to Blue who stood at the rail with the slack line at his feet, a huge grin on his face as he played the fish. With one fish aboard the mood was lighter and we enjoyed the battle and cheered for him. The fish jumped several times taking the slack line from the deck as it ran, but Blue sensed its need and allowed it its head. Once the run was finished he slowly regained the lost line. It took fifteen more minutes before the fish succumbed and floated belly up on the surface. We hauled it aboard and exchanged grins at the the fresh food we would have for dinner and the future that lay ahead.

Made in United States
Troutdale, OR
10/08/2024

23542320R00137